Paintbrushes and Arrows

M.C. Finotti

Pineapple Press, Inc.
Sarasota, Florida

Inquiries should be addressed to:

Pineapple Press, Inc.
P.O. Box 3889
Sarasota, Florida 34230

www.pineapplepress.com

Library of Congress Cataloging-in-Publication Data

Names: Finotti, M. C., author.
Title: Paintbrushes and arrows / by M.C. Finotti.
Description: Sarasota, FL : Pineapple Press, [2016] | Summary: In 1875, a
    nine-year-old Comanche girl, brought to the Castillo de San Marcos, a fort
    in in St. Augustine, Florida, for "re-education," bonds with a
    fourteen-year-old white girl who teaches art classes to the prisoners.
Identifiers: LCCN 2016014798 (print) | LCCN 2016034084 (ebook) | ISBN
    9781561649631 (pbk.) | ISBN 9781561649686
Subjects: LCSH: Castillo de San Marcos (Saint Augustine, Fla.)--History--19th
    century--Juvenile fiction. | Comanche Indians--Juvenile fiction. | CYAC:
    Castillo de San Marcos (Saint Augustine, Fla.)--Fiction. | Comanche
    Indians--Fiction. | Indians of North America--Great Plains--Fiction. |
    Art--Fiction. | Prisons--Fiction. | Saint Augustine (Fla.)--History--19th
    century--Fiction.
Classification: LCC PZ7.F49845 Pai 2016 (print) | LCC PZ7.F49845 (ebook) |
    DDC [Fic]--dc23
LC record available at https://lccn.loc.gov/2016014798

First Edition
10 9 8 7 6 5 4 3 2 1

Printed and bound in the USA

Chapter 1

Ah-kah, May 18, 1875

Ah-kah twisted a piece of fringe into a knot. It was the fourth knot she'd made at the bottom of her buckskin dress, each representing another day aboard the train. She sighed, wondering how many more knots she would make before this journey's end.

Ah-kah looked up to see her mother's chin bobbing above her chest. Peonte's eyes were closed, her sleek black hair covering the corners of her face. The girl worried about the dark circles ringing her mother's eyes. Was she really asleep?

"Your ashcakes and buffalo meat would taste so good right now," Ah-kah whispered. Peonte cracked open her eyes and raised her head, rewarding her daughter with a faint smile. "At least they would not be salty." Ah-kah laughed in spite of herself, wondering yet again why the Pale Face ate such salty food.

Food was always on her mind, it seemed. In the Oklahoma Territory, on land the Pale Face said her tribe must live, there had not been enough food and Ah-kah was always hungry.

Now, because the U.S. Army fed them, there was enough food; it just tasted terrible.

Ah-kah was not alone in her constant thoughts of food. It was the source of much chatter among the seventy-two Natives on the train with her. There were Cheyenne, Arapaho, Caddo, Kiowa, and Comanche, all prisoners, all bound from Fort Sill in Oklahoma to Fort Marion in St. Augustine, Florida. When the army tried to put her father, Black Horse, a Comanche chief, on the train in Fort Sill, her mother had screamed and cried and refused to let go of him. Peonte pitched such a fit that the Pale Face chief, Lieutenant Richard Pratt, allowed Peonte and Ah-kah to board the train too and travel with Black Horse and the others to Florida.

She and her mother were not officially prisoners, but they might as well have been. When the train made stops in places with hard-to-pronounce names like St. Louis, Nashville, Atlanta, and Macon, they were not allowed to get off the train. No one was.

Soon they would arrive at the end of the line, a place called Jacksonville. Ah-kah stared out the window, thinking of what she had seen along the way. There were places where buildings covered every inch of ground and sky. These places smelled bitter and had black bits of dirt falling from the sky. If she held her hand out the train car window she could even catch some. And she had seen more Pale Face than she knew existed. They walked through the train cars at every stop, bringing their terrible smell and awful stares that made Ah-kah feel so uncomfortable.

Her mother was convinced the army would hang the men once they arrived in Florida. Ah-kah could tell that Black Horse, seated beside her, was worried about this too, although he tried not to show it. Still, his eyes no longer flashed with the fierceness that sometimes scared even his daughter. By allowing the Pale Face to put him on this train, Ah-kah wondered if her father had given up a part of himself he might not get back again.

There was one other non-prisoner traveling with them, a Black man named Dick who'd been captured long ago by another chief on the train, a Kiowa named Lone Wolf. Dick spoke English, Kiowa, and, most importantly, Comanche. It was the only language common to the five tribes traveling to St. Augustine. He'd become their translator.

"They want to teach you to live like them," said Dick, explaining why he thought the army would not hang the men once they arrived in St. Augustine.

"What does that mean?" Black Horse demanded.

Dick frowned. "They don't want to kill you. They want to teach you to read and write and speak their language. They want you to learn a skill, like blacksmithing, so you can have jobs and earn money when you return home."

This set off an angry discussion among the men. No one believed Dick because no one believed what the Pale Face said. The discussion alarmed the soldiers guarding the train cars, who refused to let anyone talk anymore.

Ah-kah couldn't understand why the Pale Face wanted to teach the men skills. Didn't they already have skills? They could shoot an arrow straight through a running buffalo. They could make axes from stones. They could tame wild ponies. Without these skills her people could not survive.

Ah-kah sat quietly, listening for the train's occasional whistle. It reminded her of Kaku's sweet singing. She worried about her grandmother and prayed that the Great Spirit would bring her enough food to fill her belly.

She tried to think of running alongside a cool stream, her

thick braids bouncing on her back. But her thoughts were interrupted when a Kiowa seated behind her coughed a deep, wet cough. She turned to see Wolf Stomach slumped against the train car, looking very weak. His brother, Toothless, tried to hand him a tin cup of water, but Wolf Stomach shook his head. He would not take it.

Ah-kah sighed and turned back around. She caught her father's eye. "When will we get there?" she whispered.

Black Horse just shook his head.

Chapter 2

Callie, May 21, 1875

Painting felt like freedom to me. I hated to be interrupted. Even so, I gave in to James' constant pleading and left my easel and watercolors in the backyard, where I'd been blissfully painting palm fronds in variant shades of Hooker's Green, No. 1.

I allowed my little brother to pull me down narrow St. George Street, through the old city gate and over to Fort Marion, the ancient fort built by the Spanish nearly two centuries ago. I could see it clearly from my bedroom window, sitting low and squat on a bluff overlooking Matanzas Bay.

James wanted us both to witness the arrival of a group of Plains Indians to our antique town. Some two hundred townspeople were already there, chatting, laughing, and looking eagerly down the street for the wagons from Toccoi. Like most visitors to St. Augustine, the Natives had arrived by train in Jacksonville, a city to the north of us, the day before. They'd taken a steamer down the St. Johns River to Toccoi, where they boarded wagons for the eighteen-mile trip east to our tiny town by the sea.

James disappeared into the crowd the moment we arrived, which I found irritating. He'd dragged me here, after all. A man passed by selling sweets while another held up copies of the *Tri-Weekly* for sale. The carnival-like atmosphere of the crowd perturbed me. Weren't these thieves and murderers arriving in our town? Why was everyone celebrating?

Someone yelled my name. "Callie!"

I knew it must be Ben, and I stood on my tiptoes to try and spot his head of brown curls somewhere in the crowd. To my great surprise I found him waving from atop a thick branch of a wide oak tree. I ran to the tree and Ben offered me his hand. I grabbed it, noticing in an instant how warm and strong it felt against mine.

"Why are you up there?" I asked as I placed my foot between a low joining of two trunks.

"Great view," said Ben, pulling me up into the branches where I immediately met his bright blue eyes. Their sparkle always startled me even though I'd been looking into that same pair of eyes since I was three.

I'd hardly settled myself into the treetop when a wagon rounded a bend in the street, pulled by four horses. The bed of the wagon was covered by a large white tarp with the letters "U.S." printed boldly on the side. As the wagon passed underneath us, I noticed a toothy alligator skull tied to its end gate.

I pointed to it. "What's that for?"

"To showcase the wild nature of the passengers, I'd imagine," Ben said.

The wagon stopped close to the tree and two soldiers jumped down. They refused to talk to anyone as they pushed their way through the crowd that now swelled around them.

"Make way. Stand back." The townspeople squished together, creating a tiny pathway for the soldiers to the end gate.

Seconds later the first Native staggered out of the wagon, loaded down with chains. The only sound was the clinking of metal that bound the man's wrists and ankles. He refused to make eye contact with anyone. Instead, he focused on something in the distance far above the crowd.

Townspeople reached out to touch him, and I was not surprised to see James and his friend Willie among them. White hands felt the Native's coal black braids, his skin the color of burnt sienna, his fringed leather pants in rich cadmium brown. Eleven more Natives followed closely behind, all chained together. Clearly, the army was taking no chances.

I couldn't help but notice that every Native wore a piece of cotton cloth hanging from the front of his pants while another cloth of exactly the same color hung from his pants around back. Many wore earrings and beaded chokers of primary colors. All wore leather moccasins.

As a soldier directed the group up the small hill toward the fort, I was surprised to find the Natives not nearly as fearsome as I'd imagined. There were no scalps of white settlers hanging from their belts. Instead they appeared skinny and weak.

"They don't look well," I said.

Ben nodded in agreement.

Another wagon soon arrived and a second group of twelve climbed out the end gate. Soldiers escorted these Natives through the crowd toward the fort. This time, however, the man selling newspapers approached a wiry Native almost directly below us. He identified himself as a columnist with the *Tri-Weekly*.

"Are you the Comanche leader Black Horse?" he asked.

The Native ignored him but the columnist would not give up. "Black Horse, is it true you…"

The man named Black Horse stopped and turned, his eyes flashing. I could see a large vein throbbing in his neck. The spindly newspaperman no doubt saw it too because he took a step back. Just then a young Indian woman jumped out of the wagon and rushed toward Black Horse.

"Po-ka-do-ah! Po-ka-do-ah!" she screamed, sobbing. The hushed crowd watched, enthralled.

A Native girl about the same age as James followed the woman. I assumed she was the girl's mother. Both wore leather dresses, fringed and beaded. A soldier with an angry red scar on his cheek shoved the mother and daughter out of the way. "Get back," he growled. The woman stumbled to the ground as another soldier shoved Black Horse toward the fort. The little girl tended to her mother.

I gasped. "Are they that man's wife and child?"

Ben shrugged. "I think so."

Black Horse walked toward the fort, his jaw tightly clenched. The little girl, meanwhile, wrapped the woman in a consoling hug.

Surely, I was not a big supporter of these Native peoples— they scared me too much for that—but I never expected to see a Native woman crying before me in such anguish and a young girl bravely trying to comfort her mother.

Just then Lieutenant Richard Pratt, the man in charge of the fort, approached the soldier with the scar. The lieutenant's dark blue jacket was buttoned tightly despite the heat. "Take Peonte and Ah-kah and go to the fort, Sergeant. They can stay there."

The soldier nodded and motioned with the butt of his rifle

to tell the pair to move. The little girl helped her mother up. The mother was still sobbing.

Ben kept count as more prisoners arrived at Fort Marion. Much to my surprise there was another woman among them, also wearing a fringed and beaded leather dress. She too wore moccasins, but her legs were wrapped in bright red cloth, making the chains around her ankles all the more visible. She wore a blanket over her shoulders.

"Who is that?" I wondered.

Ben frowned as he stared at the woman. "I think that's Buffalo Calf. She's Cheyenne. I read about her in the newspaper. She and her husband, Medicine Water, murdered a family of settlers called the Germans. Medicine Water is supposed to be here too."

I had never seen a murderess before. Like most of the Natives, she wore her hair in two long braids. She appeared thin but sturdy as she shuffled toward the fort. On the way there, she pulled the blanket over her head.

By the time the last Native climbed out of a wagon, Ben had counted seventy-two prisoners. We'd also seen one Negro man dressed like a Native, but since he was not in chains we did not think him a prisoner.

Ben climbed out of the tree and reached up to help me down. The arrival of the Natives perplexed me. "How long are they meant to stay here?"

Ben shook his head. "No one has said."

"And tell me again. Why exactly are they here in St. Augustine?"

"It's Lieutenant Pratt's bold experiment. He wants to kill the Native but save the man by teaching him new ways."

I was still trying to imagine what the army would actually teach the Natives at the fort when James and Willie joined us.

"Did you see that?" James asked, his freckled cheeks flushed from both the afternoon sun and the excitement of the arrival.

"It was interesting," I admitted as I started to walk home, the boys following.

Willie, two years older than James and not always the best influence, brimmed with opinions. "Did you see that Native with the long hair and the big necklace? That was Medicine Water."

"That describes half the men on the train," Ben scoffed.

Willie answered with certainty. "He was the one with the murderous look in his eye."

Ben chuckled dismissively. "You've been reading too many dime novels," he said of the books that James and his friend adored. They featured a lot of fighting between Natives and frontiersmen, as well as Natives and army soldiers.

But my little brother hung on Willie's every word. "I bet if he had a tomahawk he would have attacked someone," James said. I tried to steer the conversation in a more peaceful direction. "Well at least these Natives seem to value cleanliness."

The three looked at me, confused. I hurried to explain myself. "Those cotton towels hanging from their waistbands. They use them to keep their hands clean, no doubt."

The corners of Ben's mouth twitched up and down. James snickered. Willie slapped his leg and laughed loudly. "Those weren't towels," Willie practically yelled at me.

James burst out laughing. "They're breechcloths."

The three enjoyed much merriment at my expense. I quickened my pace. I did not find the matter the least bit funny, especially when Ben stopped laughing long enough to explain that a breechcloth is essentially a Native's undergarment. What I had thought were two towels tucked neatly into the front and back of a Native's waistband was actually one long piece of cloth that ran between his legs and was held in place by a leather cord around his waist. The excess cloth hung down like a towel outside his leggings in both the front and back.

After James explained that some Natives chose not to use a cloth at all, but fur pelts sewn together instead, my humiliation was complete.

I walked even faster, eager to return to my painting.

"Where are you going?" called Ben, still chuckling.

"Home," I called back. "I graduate in less than a week. I have things to do that are far more important than this!"

"If you need any towels," Willie yelled, "I know where you can find some!" And their laughter started up all over again.

Chapter 3

Ah-kah, May 28, 1875

For Ah-kah, the food at the fort was hardly much better than the food on the train. She lined up for breakfast, tin plate and cup in hand, to be served by soldier cooks. The morning biscuits were hard and cold, same as on the train, although now there was some salty gray gravy to soften them. The rest of the meals were not much better.

Since arriving at the fort, Ah-kah, admittedly, had eaten one thing she enjoyed greatly. It was shaped like a half moon and about the same color. It had a thick skin that once peeled away revealed a sweet fruit inside. The Pale Face called it a banana.

Still, Ah-kah longed to walk in the woods and bring back some real food—berries or squirrels or fish. But such a walk was impossible here because Peonte would not allow her to leave the fort.

"These Pale Face are crazy," said Peonte, simply and utterly convinced of the truth of her words. "You will stay right beside me where I know you are safe."

Ah-kah sighed, frustrated. Back in the village she was allowed much freedom once her chores were done. She could play with her cousins, swim in the river, or run with her dog, Sundance. Now she was a prisoner just like her father and the other men.

Still, soon after she arrived Ah-kah managed to get away from her mother long enough to explore the fort, which included climbing up stone steps to an area called "the ramparts." Ah-kah had never seen such a tall staircase before and found it thrilling to climb the steps—up and down, over and over again. She'd rest at the top on the ramparts when she got tired, enjoying the cool breezes and the view of the town beyond—a town Ah-kah wondered if she'd ever get to see close up.

The fort contained many small rooms located off the courtyard that were connected one to the other. Ah-kah quickly realized she could walk practically all the way around the fort just by walking from one room to the next.

One day during her first week at the fort, she found a room lined with benches, six on each side. There was a wooden cross on one wall and a doorway not far away from it that led to a short hallway. Ah-kah stepped through the doorway and into the short hall, wondering where it led. It was lit by one narrow rectangular window that had been covered by a large spider web. The web hung from the window like a lace curtain, which were so loved by the Pale Face. Ah-kah crept down the corridor, ready to run back out if necessary.

The corridor soon turned to the right and Ah-kah stopped, wondering whether to continue. She wasn't scared, but she had a pretty good idea she wasn't allowed in this part of the fort. A fat, black animal suddenly shot past her. Ah-kah knew it wasn't a dog, but she wasn't sure what exactly it was.

She peered around the corner to see where the animal had come from and saw a brick wall that stretched down from the ceiling. Oddly, it stopped about three feet from the clay floor, leaving a narrow opening.

Ah-kah knelt down and stuck her head into the opening. There, on the other side, she saw a small square room lit by a torch. A door made from iron bars stood open on one side of the room. A Native lay curled on a cot nearby. Who was that? Ah-kah wondered. She turned her head in the opposite direction and saw a soldier sitting on a stool, whittling. The soldier, sensing her presence, looked up.

"Hey!" he yelled.

Ah-kah darted out of the opening, thankful she did not hit her head. She bolted down the corridor as fast as that animal she'd seen moments before. She did not stop running until she was back in the courtyard where the sunshine hurt her eyes after the darkness of the hallway.

Ah-kah knew she had seen the prison room. The Pale Face had kept her father locked inside one back at Fort Sill. But she felt confused. Wasn't this fort supposed to be different? The men were here to learn new ways. But how would they learn new ways if they were to be treated the same as before? And who was that in the prison room with the soldier anyway?

Ah-kah found her mother seated in the shade, her back against a wall. She almost asked Peonte about the prisoner behind the iron bars, but stopped. What if her mother thought exploring the fort was too dangerous? What if she really did force Ah-kah to sit by her side all day?

Peonte smiled weakly. "I have news that will make you happy."

"The army is taking us home?" Ah-kah asked as she slid her back down the wall to sit beside her mother.

Peonte shook her head. "The men asked if they could wash in the river tomorrow. The Pale Face chief said yes. Do you want to go?"

Ah-kah nodded eagerly. Just then her father joined them, looking cross. "Wolf Stomach is in the prison room. They put him there to keep him away from the rest of us, even his brother Toothless. They don't want him to make anyone else sick."

So that's who it was, Ah-kah thought. Peonte, meanwhile, shook her head and frowned. "He needs a healer. Not a jailer."

Ah-kah dared not move. Her mother and father did not usually talk about important things in front of her and she did not want them to stop.

"The Pale Face healer says Wolf Stomach will meet the Great Spirit soon."

Ah-kah felt sad when she heard this. She wondered what his brother would do without him.

That night, she did not sleep well, wondering whether Wolf Stomach had passed into the next world yet. When the army's 5:30 A.M. bugle announced it was time to get up, Ah-kah was already awake. So was Peonte.

The two gathered with the men in the courtyard for the trip to the river. Soldiers directed them toward the "sally port." Ah-kah had no idea what a "sally port" was, but found the name quite fun to say. Once there, she realized it was simply a short tunnel leading up to the fort's front gates.

Ah-kah walked through the fort's gates and felt a smile spread across her face. This was freedom, she thought, to have the earth and sky open before her without any walls in the way.

A hint of sunrise peeked through the horizon to the east as Ah-kah skipped down the bluff to the river, her mother not far behind.

Ah-kah could not stop staring at the strange trees that spotted the landscape. They had long skinny trunks, no arms to speak of, and leaves that grew only at the top, spikey and green like a tassel. Ah-kah thought them quite ugly.

The men wasted no time wading into the water wearing only their breechcloths. Ah-kah thought about joining them.

She turned to ask her mother's permission when she noticed a Pale Face girl seated on the ground on the far side of the fort. The girl looked to be a few winters older than Ah-kah. She was painting something on a piece of paper that lay atop a small box on her lap.

Ah-kah pulled her mother's arm. She wanted to get closer to the girl. Peonte nodded and the two walked closer. The girl's hair, which spilled carelessly from her hat, was the same bright yellow color that she was using to paint the sunrise. Her long, slender fingers held a paintbrush, probably made from squirrel hairs, Ah-kah thought.

In addition to the yellow in the girl's painting, there were streaks of blue, pink, and purple in it too, just like in the morning sky. Ah-kah itched to try painting that herself.

Suddenly the men behind her began to yell. Ah-kah turned to see them grabbing handfuls of clay off the river bottom and painting it on each other, laughing. She turned back to see the girl startled, looking fearfully at the men.

Ah-kah wanted to tell the girl that no one would hurt her.

She was trying to figure out a way to do this when the girl noticed Ah-kah and Peonte standing close by. Alarmed, the girl jumped up. In the process she knocked over a jar of water and some flat shells that contained dried paint colors. Ah-kah found those shells interesting. Back home, paint was kept in bags made from tanned buffalo hides. The box that had been perched on the girl's lap fell to the ground, spilling a stack of clean white paper.

Ah-kah reached down to help gather the paper and picked up the painting the girl had been working on. It was still damp. She handed it to the girl, but the girl backed away, shaking her head. Her arms were full of paper and paint and the paintbrush, which she gripped tightest of all. The Pale Face girl said not a word. She just ran past Ah-kah and Peonte, leaving Ah-kah holding the wet painting.

Ah-kah stared at the sunrise on the paper. She would have liked to watch the Pale Face girl finish it.

Chapter 4

Callie, June 7, 1875

I buried my nose in a bouquet of magnolia blossoms, inhaling their lemony scent.

"Thank you, Mrs. Broderick. Magnolias are my favorite." Ben's mother hugged me close as Ben stood by respectfully.

"I know, dear. They were Neeley's favorite too."

I swallowed hard at the mention of my mother's name. I had dreamed of her just that morning, the two of us sitting cozily on the loveseat in our parlor, a sketchbook open before us. Mother stretched out her hand. "Hands are wonderful to draw, Callie, when you can't think of anything else. Give each finger three sections, except the thumb, of course." She bent her thumb to show me it had just two joints.

I wanted to sit by Mother's side sketching forever, but when I turned over in bed the dream was gone. Just like my mother. She died in childbirth the night James was born. Now, some nine years later, it was my graduation day.

Mrs. Broderick cupped my chin with her hand. "Neeley

would have been so proud of you."

I hugged her again, and smiled sadly.

Just then Mr. Newman called all five of us graduates to the front of the room to begin the festivities. I think half the town had showed up for our grand doing, which was to begin with each graduate demonstrating their best accomplishment.

Lina Walker stepped forward first. She fanned herself with a new, indigo-colored fan, showing it off. The fan matched the sash on her white dress perfectly. She read a composition about the next decade and how it was a bright one for us girls. I didn't believe for a second she wrote it, especially when she read the part about how she might become a missionary in India someday. Lina Walker would be hard pressed to find India on a map, if you asked me. Still, her mother clapped loudly from the audience.

Ada Parker went next. She played a selection on an upright piano that had been wheeled into the schoolhouse for the occasion. Sarah Barnett and Elizabeth Wigand, both well practiced in the art of stitchery, followed Ada. They showed off a lovely quilt they'd made together and explained its complicated pattern called Ocean Waves.

Then it was my turn. I stepped to the front of the room and clasped my hands together behind my back so no one could see them tremble. I stood beside an easel my father and James had brought over earlier. There was a painting on the easel covered with a cloth.

I tried to explain my painting, but my voice croaked. I cleared my throat and began again. "This is a painting I made for the schoolhouse. I thought you might display it here, Mr. Newman, if you see fit."

I pulled off the cover and held my breath, waiting to see the crowd's reaction. The audience collectively leaned forward to see the new St. Augustine Lighthouse, white with its encircling black stripe standing tall against a cloudless blue sky. The lighthouse had opened earlier this year, replacing an old one built by the Spanish centuries before that had all but fallen into the sea.

Ben started clapping and everyone joined him. Mr. Newman rushed up to thank me. I started breathing again.

Mr. Newman handed each of us our diploma and we all enjoyed refreshments. Our housekeeper, Dominga, had baked a delicious spice cake with lemon icing and I couldn't wait to tell her how quickly everyone ate it up.

Mrs. Mather, an educator who owned a school of higher learning for girls in our tiny town, cornered Father and me during the refreshments. She was plump and serious with gray hair that she parted down the middle and twisted into two tight buns on either side of her head.

"Your painting is lovely, Callison."

"Thank you, Mrs. Mather," I bowed, smiling to myself. No one but the ever-precise Mrs. Mather called me by my real name.

She turned to Father. "Will you be enrolling Callison in my school this fall, Dr. Crump?"

"I'm not sure, Sarah. Callie plans to apply to the Pennsylvania Academy of Fine Arts in Philadelphia next year when she turns fifteen. Her mother went there, you know."

Mrs. Mather nodded. "The value of a Northern education cannot be underestimated." Mrs. Mather was from Connecticut and one of the first women to graduate from Mount Holyoke College in Massachusetts.

Father nodded and appeared ready to move on when Mrs. Mather peered at us through her spectacles.

"I don't know if you've heard, but I'm to teach the Native captives how to read and write."

Father smiled. "That is excellent news, Mrs. Mather. You have a genius for instruction."

Mrs. Mather smiled. "I was thinking that perhaps Callison would like to work with me. Teaching is a wonderful profession for young women."

I shuddered as my mind raced to the Natives I'd seen outside the fort not long ago, especially the mother and daughter who'd snuck up behind me and stood there watching me paint for who knows how long. I planned to keep my distance from these Natives as much as possible. After all, I'd heard those stories of young girls on the frontier captured and forced to live like Natives for years before they were rescued or escaped.

Father put my feelings into words. "Do you think it would be safe?"

Mrs. Mather tossed her head and huffed. "Of course. Soldiers from the U.S. Army will guard us." She squared her shoulders. "I welcome the opportunity to educate these wild peoples."

I did not feel the same way and thought I had the perfect excuse. "Surely there are churchwomen with more experience, Mrs. Mather. I've never taught reading and writing before."

"Of course there are churchwomen to teach that," she snapped. "But you can draw and paint. I want you to teach sketch work."

My jaw dropped. I glanced at Father. He looked equally surprised. And then Mrs. Mather said the very thing she knew neither of us could dispute. "I daresay if Neeley were still alive she'd be at that fort teaching sketch work tomorrow!"

Father and I exchanged a look. Indeed, my mother, Cornelia

Callison Crump, would have helped any way she could. There was no way in good conscience I could deny Mrs. Mather's request. I swallowed hard and managed to croak that I might be able to find a little time.

"Wonderful!" Mrs. Mather smiled broadly and walked away. Before retreating entirely, she stopped and barked her final orders. "I'll see you at the fort this Monday, Callison. Bring some art supplies. And bring a plan. A good teacher always has a plan ready for the day's lesson!"

She left me speechless. Monday was just two days away. Even Father seemed amazed. "Now that's a woman who knows how to get what she wants," he said.

Chapter 5

Ah-kah, May 28, 1875

Ah-kah brought the Pale Face girl's painting back to the fort and placed it beside her blanket. Peonte frowned when she saw it, but Ah-kah didn't care. She considered it her own little bit of sunshine in this otherwise dreary fort.

Ah-kah worried she wouldn't be allowed outside the fort again for a long time, but those worries turned out to be misplaced. The very next day, after yet another breakfast of hard biscuits and salty gravy, Ah-kah noticed Dick walking purposely toward the sally port.

She ran to catch up to him. "Where are you going?"

He stopped. "To walk around the town. Do you want to come?"

Ah-kah smiled, realizing she was as free to leave the fort as Dick was, providing her mother would allow her to leave. Dick agreed to wait while she ran to ask.

Ah-kah found her parents sitting side by side in the shade, looking forlorn. "Can I go outside the fort with Dick?" she asked.

Peonte shook her head. "You have no money, no reason to go out there."

Ah-kah stomped her foot, anger growing in her chest. "I am not a prisoner."

Peonte did not blink.

Suddenly, Black Horse spoke. "You may go."

Peonte turned to look at him, an eyebrow raised.

"She must learn to get along with the Pale Face," he said. "We all must. Or we will die."

Her father's words made her victory seem hollow. Still, determined to take advantage of this unexpected freedom, Ah-kah ran to find Dick, who was waiting beside the fort's now-open gate. The smile on her face told Dick all he needed to know. Together they walked out onto the bluff.

"Be back before sundown," a soldier told them as he closed the gates behind them.

"What did he say?" Ah-kah asked, feeling a stab of doubt as she watched the gates close.

"We must return before the sun sets," Dick explained in Comanche.

Ah-kah looked at Dick nervously. He hurried to reassure her. "We won't be gone that long. They'll let us back in."

Ah-kah took a deep breath and turned her attention toward town. As they walked down the bluff, she noticed a wagon pass before her, pulled by two slow and very sad-looking horses, nothing like the spirited ponies her father once owned.

She and Dick crossed a dusty street and walked down a narrow lane filled with tall houses sitting behind white wooden fences. Ah-kah wondered if anyone ever felt comfortable inside those stiff boxes.

She enjoyed seeing the colorful flowers that grew in front

of every house, especially the bright yellow flowers with droopy heads that were taller than she was. The abundance of flowers reminded her of the prairie back home, with flowers so plentiful they perfumed the air with their sweetness. But Ah-kah was determined not to feel sad on this walk. She followed Dick to the end of the lane. He turned onto a busy street and climbed onto a wide walkway made of pine boards. Ah-kah stopped, unsure if she should follow.

"It's okay," Dick called. "The Pale Face use these walkways so their shoes don't get muddy when it rains."

Ah-kah had never heard of such a thing. She scrambled up the stairs and followed Dick. They passed a very large white building with a cross atop it, the same sort of cross Ah-kah had seen in a room at the fort. The front door to this building was wide open and Ah-kah could see a statue deep inside of a woman wearing a bright blue cloth on her head. The woman held a baby lovingly in her arms. Ah-kah thought it quite beautiful.

Dick called to her. "Ah-kah! Stay close."

She ran to catch up. A Pale Face on the walkway stopped to stare openly at Ah-kah in her buckskin dress and moccasins. She did not like all the attention and was relieved when they crossed another dusty street and found themselves atop a stone seawall, the river not far below them. The fort was to their left, but they walked away from it. Ah-kah enjoyed the cool breeze off the water. They passed an area where many boats were tied up to a wooden walkway, a walkway that extended out into the river.

In time the seawall ended and Ah-kah and Dick stood staring at a wall of tall reedy plants. Ah-kah suddenly had an idea.

"Do you think those reeds would make good arrows?"

Ah-kah did not know how to shoot with a bow and arrow. Only boys did that back home, but she had always wanted to learn. Now, she decided, was the perfect time. After all, Black Horse was one of the best bowmen in the Comanche nation. Maybe he would teach her. If not, there were plenty of other Natives to ask.

"Only one way to find out," Dick said as he hopped off the seawall, his feet sinking in the mud. Dick pulled one foot out of the muck and stepped slowly forward until he was close enough to grasp one of the tall reeds at its base. He pulled. It did not budge.

"I'll find something to cut it with," Ah-kah called out helpfully. She cast about until her eyes landed on a long oyster shell along the riverbank. Ah-kah lay down on the seawall and managed to grab the shell without getting her feet in the muck.

She threw it to Dick who used it to hack at the reeds. He eventually cut off a few of the tall plants and walked back slowly through the muck to the seawall, handing Ah-kah the reeds.

They felt light and strong in her hands.

"They'll make good arrows, I think," she said, smiling at Dick, who smiled back. He stopped to rinse his feet in the river and then the two walked back toward the fort atop the seawall.

"What will you use for a bow?" Dick asked.

Ah-kah shrugged. She had no idea.

"I saw a tree on the other side of the fort. I think it was a mulberry," Dick said.

Ah-kah knew bendable mulberry branches made fine strong bows, and when Dick offered to climb the tree, she eagerly waited for him below.

Dick was soon lost high in the tree's leafy canopy, where he insisted the best branches for bows could be found. Ah-kah bent back her head and watched him saw away at a branch with the oyster shell.

While she waited, she noticed two boys walking across the field toward her. As they got closer, Ah-kah noticed one boy had red speckles on his face the color of the dirt back in the Oklahoma Territory. The other boy seemed taller and older, with straight brown hair and a bumpy nose. Ah-kah thought he looked mean.

Bumpy Nose stopped in front of Ah-kah and looked her straight in the eye. She matched his gaze.

"Hey, James," he said. "Did I ever tell you what my daddy says about Injuns?"

Spotted Face said nothing, but that didn't stop the other one from answering the question he'd just asked. "He says, 'The only good Injun is a dead Injun.'"

Ah-kah could not understand what the boys were saying, but it did not sound nice. She stood very still, watching them carefully.

Suddenly, there was a rustle. Dick jumped down from the tree, startling the boys.

"I think I hear your mother calling you," Dick spoke quietly, his voice low and throaty.

The older boy smiled. "I don't hear nothing. Do you, James?"

The younger boy wanted no trouble. He grabbed the older boy's arm. "Come on, Willie. Let's go." He pulled the boy toward town.

Ah-kah immediately asked Dick what the boys had said, but Dick would not tell her. Instead he gathered the branches, a deep frown creasing his brow, and walked purposefully up the hill to the fort. Ah-kah knew the boys had said something unkind, and this worried her. Not because she was scared of them, mind you, but because Dick might tell Peonte, and her mother would certainly never let her leave the fort again.

Ah-kah begged Dick not to tell her parents.

Dick frowned and looked back down the bluff. "They are bad boys, Ah-kah. You must not leave this fort alone. Will you promise me that?"

The girl nodded solemnly, and together they walked back through the fort's thick wooden gates.

Chapter 6

Callie, June 9, 1875

Whenever anyone talked about opportunities for girls they always mentioned teaching. But I did not want to teach. I wanted to do something far less ordinary, like travel to New York City to create illustrations for *Harper's Magazine* or attend art school in Philadelphia.

Yet, here I was trudging up the hill to Fort Marion, twin boxes of paint and paper under my arms. I considered it a cruel twist of fate that I was heading there to teach. I planned to perform this duty precisely once in order to appease Mrs. Mather and rid myself of any guilt she had made me feel.

Mrs. Mather waited for me near the sally port. "Lieutenant Pratt is going to address us."

We hurried across the fort's dusty interior courtyard to a small chapel decorated with simple benches and a large wooden cross. About a dozen St. Augustine ladies were already there. I sat beside Mrs. Gibbs, one of mother's dearest friends, herself a former teacher.

"I daresay the air in here is horrid," she whispered. I looked around to see dark, furry mold blanketing part of the room like wallpaper. I nodded in agreement and gathered my skirt in close.

Mrs. Mather stood before us. "Ladies, I'd like to introduce you to the man responsible for bringing the Natives here, Lieutenant Richard Henry Pratt." She clapped her gloved hands together and we all clapped too as Lieutenant Pratt stepped forward, his hat tucked snugly under his arm.

"Thank you for participating in this bold experiment," the lieutenant said. "Many of these captives were leaders in their tribes, some of the most dangerous Natives on the Great Plains."

Lieutenant Pratt looked at each of us. "It is my hope that we can remove the treachery they arrived with and turn each and every one of them into a contributing member of society."

Mrs. Mather led us in clapping once again. Lieutenant Pratt continued. "They were born a blank slate, just like you and me. It was their environment that shaped them into what they are today, and it is our environment that will reshape them. Together we will work to reconstruct these Natives. Simply put, ladies: By teaching them how to live in our world we will save their lives."

Mrs. Mather clapped enthusiastically and again we joined her. She stepped to the front and introduced each of us to the lieutenant. I stood as she called my name. "Callison Crump was practically born with a paintbrush in her hand. I've recruited her to teach art classes to the Natives."

Lieutenant Pratt offered a kind smile. "There is a long and proud tradition among these Natives of recording their lives in pictures. I think you'll find some industrious artists here."

"Yes sir," I murmured and sat back down, thinking I'd better

M.C. Finotti

get a good look at those artists today, because I wasn't coming back here ever again to see them.

After the introductions, Lieutenant Pratt led us back to the courtyard, where I was shocked to see the Natives lined up, standing at attention like army soldiers. Gone were the chains and shackles, the moccasins, the fringed leggings, and certainly the breechcloths I'd seen when they arrived. Instead each Native was dressed like a soldier in hard shoes, gray pants, and a dark blue jacket. But perhaps most surprisingly, their long hair was gone, chopped off just below their ears, further accentuating the dramatic cheekbones so typical of their race.

Mrs. Mather bustled past me and sat on a low stool beside a makeshift desk that appeared to be an ammunition crate turned on its end. A ledger book sat atop it.

Lieutenant Pratt walked among the Natives and divided them into small groups. He walked each group over to Mrs. Mather, where she was now accompanied by the Negro man I recognized from the depot. He too was no longer dressed in Native garb, but wore beige pants and a homespun shirt.

The first captive said his name. "Ma-ha-ih-ha-chit."

The Negro man, whose name I soon learned was Dick, repeated the captive's name in English. "He is Little Medicine. He is Cheyenne." Mrs. Mather wrote down the native's name in the ledger book.

Another native stepped forward. "Zo-pe-he."

Dick translated. "His name is Toothless." I smiled to myself because, indeed, this Native was missing his two front teeth.

Once five names were written down, Mrs. Mather called a teacher and wrote her name at the top of the page. Then a soldier led the entire group to a classroom. Lessons were to begin right away.

I was nervous by the time it was my turn to receive my students. But I took a deep breath and told myself it would all be over soon. The first Native in my group stepped forward. He whispered his name.

"E-tah-dle-un."

"Boy Hunting," Dick translated. "He's Kiowa."

Boy Hunting's smooth chin bore not a bit of hair. Mrs. Mather wrote his name in the book and looked up expectantly for my next student, who soon stepped forward, his large hands hanging limply by his sides. He moved with an economy of motion.

"Oak-un-hat-uh."

"Making Medicine," Dick translated. "Can also mean Yellow Paint. He's Cheyenne."

I thought Yellow Paint a perfect name for an artist, but Mrs. Mather apparently preferred his other name. I watched her dutifully write "Making Medicine" in the ledger book.

The next Native stepped forward and glared at Mrs. Mather, refusing to volunteer his name.

"Your name?" she demanded.

He growled something at her in his native tongue. Mrs. Mather appeared unfazed. Dick intervened, exchanging words with him. The Native frowned and finally barked his name.

"Isa-tah."

Dick translated. "You folks call him White Horse. He's Kiowa. A war chief."

White Horse kicked the dirt as he walked away to stand with my other students.

Mrs. Mather looked at me. "You've only got three students, Callison. I asked Lieutenant Pratt to start you with a small class since you've never taught before." She nodded toward

Lieutenant Pratt, who was to lead us to our classroom.

Mrs. Mather fired some last-minute instructions at me before I walked away. "Even though you're doing artwork, teach them as many English words as you can. They need to learn English!"

Just outside my classroom, Lieutenant Pratt introduced me to a soldier who would be my guard. "This is Sergeant Falloon."

"Rhymes with balloon, Miss," said the soldier, tipping his hat to reveal a head of ginger hair.

I bowed slightly. "How do you do."

As he turned to leave, Lieutenant Pratt offered these parting words. "White Horse is having a difficult time adjusting, Miss Crump. I'm hoping art class will have a calming effect on him."

Just my luck! I swallowed hard, thinking I needed to ask Ben more about this White Horse fellow. "Yes sir," I replied, trying to sound calmer than I felt.

My classroom was about the same size as the chapel room, but thankfully it had a small rectangular window high on a wall, which made it far less damp and moldy. Five unused cannons were stacked atop each other in the back of the room; a lone barrel stood in the corner near the door, next to Falloon, who, I noted, was armed with a trusty Bowie knife and a Springfield rifle. There was just one piece of furniture, a long bench placed in the middle of the dirt floor.

"Do you want the captives to sit, Miss?"

"Oh. Yes. Of course." I admit I was nervous, unsure what to do.

Falloon motioned to the Natives to sit on the bench.

I decided to introduce myself. "My name is Callie Crump." They stared at me blankly, and I remembered they did not know much English. I thumped my chest. "CAL-ee." I felt as if I was moving in a slow dream, watching myself perform.

Sergeant Falloon offered a gentle suggestion. "Do you have something you want them to do, Miss?"

I fumbled with a latch on my paper box and grabbed three pieces of paper and three sticks of graphite from inside. Falloon helped me pass them out.

"Ajo," said Boy Hunting, when I handed him his paper and pencil. I frowned, not knowing what he'd said.

"That means, 'thank you,'" Falloon said, helpfully.

"Oh. How do I say 'you're welcome?'"

"Ajo," Falloon repeated.

"It's the same word?"

Falloon nodded.

"Ajo," I said to Boy Hunting. He smiled sadly and looked at his paper.

I asked Falloon to roll the barrel into the center of the room, and as he did I pulled three long, skinny datil peppers from my dress pocket. I had plucked them from Dominga's garden just that morning. These yellow-orange peppers were precious to her, grown from seeds her ancestors brought from Spain nearly two hundred years before. She wanted them back after the day's lesson.

I placed the peppers atop the barrel so the Natives could draw a still life. But since they couldn't understand my instructions, I thought to demonstrate what I wanted them to do. I sat before the men with the paper box balanced on my lap and began to draw the three peppers. I drew a long, narrow rectangle then softened the shape by smudging the lines with my finger. I motioned to the Natives to do the same.

Boy Hunting and Making Medicine both placed their papers on the bench and knelt down to start drawing. Chief White Horse remained on the bench. He crossed his arms tightly and refused to look at me. I thought it best to leave him alone.

I worked on my drawing a bit more and got up to see what the other students had done. Boy Hunting had already finished, a perfect still life on his paper. In fact, in the corner, he was now drawing a man dressed in Native garb sitting atop a gray speckled horse. It struck me that the drawings were in two very different styles: The peppers looked as realistic as something I myself would draw, but the rider looked more primitive, as if it were done in a Native way. I realized suddenly that Boy Hunting could draw either way, in whatever style he chose.

Just then Boy Hunting looked at me. He looked at my sketch. He shook his head as if to say his drawing was much better than mine. I was taken aback. He had just challenged my artistic abilities!

I grabbed my paper and graphite and sat down to finish my sketch. I added texture and shading to the peppers until they practically burst with life. I could feel Boy Hunting watching me closely. When I was done, I placed my paper on the bench beside his. Boy Hunting shrugged his shoulder and looked away.

Making Medicine, meanwhile, was not drawing the peppers. He drew a Native village in a primitive style with a young woman standing beside a teepee.

"They're all quite homesick, Miss," Falloon said, nodding toward Making Medicine. "Especially him. He had to leave his pregnant wife back in the Indian Territory."

I frowned. "Oh my."

Class was soon over and the Natives rose to leave. As they left, Chief White Horse grabbed a datil pepper from the display and stuffed it in his mouth.

"Falloon!" I cried. "Tell him it's hot." Not even Dominga ate an entire datil paper all at once. Falloon chuckled. "Don't worry,

Miss. They love hot peppers. Natives eat them all the time."

I watched in amazement as White Horse swallowed the pepper and smacked his lips.

"We'll be off now, Miss." Falloon led the Natives out of the classroom.

I plopped down on the bench, exhausted. I'd only been teaching an hour but it felt like days. How could anyone find this work rewarding?

When I left the fort a short time later, I was deep in thought. I needed to devise the perfect excuse to give Mrs. Mather so I'd never have to teach this dreadful class again.

Chapter 7

Ah-kah, May 29, 1875

Ah-kah dumped a pile of reeds and mulberry branches in front of her father. He was sitting in the shade staring into the distance, Peonte at his side, their backs against the fort. Black Horse looked at the pile before him.

"Will you teach me to shoot with a bow and arrow?" his daughter asked.

Black Horse looked up at Ah-kah, then picked up a mulberry branch and examined it.

"Why do you want to learn to shoot? We are prisoners here. We cannot hunt. And we will fight no more."

She nodded. "But it will help me pass the time."

Black Horse sighed. "Your bow needs to match your size and strength," he said, quietly. "You should make a short bow first and work up to a larger one."

Ah-kah looked at him eagerly. "Will you help me?"

Black Horse stood wearily. He asked Ah-kah to hold out her right arm so he could measure her arm against the branches.

After several tries, he found a match and handed it to her.

"We can go no further," he said, sitting back down beside Peonte."We need a knife to cut notches in the bow." He shook his head sadly, and Ah-kah knew it was because he no longer possessed a knife—none of the Natives did. The army had taken them.

But Ah-kah was too excited to let that stop her. She took her bow to a nice soldier. She'd heard some of the Natives call him Falloon. Using a combination of sign language and smiles Ah-kah asked him to cut notches at either end of the bow with his knife. Once he understood what she wanted, he easily carved the notches and handed the bow branch back to her. Ah-kah showed it to Black Horse, but he was no longer in a mood to help.

Peonte, however, acknowledged the notches and took Ah-kah back to the room that had been assigned to them. There she yanked several long, thin pieces of rawhide from her dress and quickly tied them together. "Your bowstring," she announced, proudly. Ah-kah smiled. It surely didn't look like any bowstring she'd see her father use back home, but maybe it would work. She tied it to the notches at either end of the bow, and together they returned to Black Horse. He was not pleased.

"You must tie only one end of string to the bow and keep it that way until you're ready to use it," he barked, irritation spilling from within. "Otherwise the bow won't stay springy."

Ah-kah smiled to herself. She thought it a good thing that her father was irritated with her. It took energy to be irritated and that meant Black Horse was showing more life than he'd shown since they arrived in Florida.

Ah-kah untied the string from one end of the bow and looked

at her father hopefully. "Can you show me how to make arrows?"

"We don't have the right wood for arrows. They must be made from cedar," Black Horse said. He looked at the pile of reeds and scoffed. "Those will not work."

Ah-kah picked up a reed, hopefully. Black Horse looked away. "Arrows must be smoked for three days in a teepee," he said. "And the wood must be seasoned for several weeks after that."

Taking pity on her daughter, Peonte again offered to help. "I'll show you a way to make arrows."

As far as Ah-kah knew, Peonte had never made arrows before, although she could make other tools, like a hoe to break up the dirt for planting. Ah-kah watched as Peonte broke a reed in two.

"Your father likes his arrows long. But this is better for you." She handed half of a reed to Ah-kah.

Peonte began rubbing one end of the reed against the fort's rough coquina wall. "This will sharpen it, since we have no steel points."

Ah-kah did the same with her half, and soon she could see a point developing at the end of her reed. She smiled at Peonte, proud of her mother's resourcefulness.

"When we are done, you must take these arrows back to the soldier who cut your bow notches. Ask him to make a notch in the end of each arrow so it will fit into the bow string."

Ah-kah did as her mother instructed, and once the two arrows were properly notched, she returned to her father and quietly asked for his help in how to shoot them.

Again, Black Horse shook his head and sounded irritated when he spoke. "Arrows need feathers to ensure they sail straight. You will never learn to shoot without them." He got up wearily and walked away. Ah-kah looked at her mother and sighed. Peonte smiled sympathetically. "Well, we must find some feathers then," she said.

This did not prove as difficult as Ah-kah initially thought it would. The very next day when she was atop the ramparts looking out over the water and wondering where she would find some feathers, Ah-kah happened to look down at her feet. There she saw a long, white feather with black and gray stripes at its tip, sitting beside her moccasin.

Ah-kah smiled joyously, grabbed the feather, and ran to show it to her parents. She knew the Great Spirit had sent it to her.

"Where's Black Horse?" Ah-kah asked, finding her mother in her normal spot in the shade, her back against he fort's wall. She was eager to fix the feather to the arrows.

"In council with the chiefs," Peonte said.

Ah-kah showed her what she had found. Peonte smiled. "It's beautiful. But I'm sorry, child. I have never put these on an arrow. You need glue, and we have no buffalo hooves to boil to make glue."

Downcast, Ah-kah knew she would have to wait for her father to return. Her mother could sense her disappointment. "You know who knows how to fix feathers to arrows? The warrior woman. The Cheyenne they call Buffalo Calf."

Ah-kah smiled. She knew just where to find the warrior woman too. Since arriving at the fort, Buffalo Calf had found a home for herself in the fort's kitchen, which Ah-kah thought an odd place for a warrior woman until she realized there were not many other places at the fort for her to go.

Ah-kah found Buffalo Calf with a rolling pin in her hands, flattening out dough at a kitchen table. She looked deep in thought. "What are you making?" Ah-kah asked.

Buffalo Calf looked up, startled. Then she looked back down at her dough. "Molasses cookies," she said quietly, working the rolling pin.

Ah-kah sensed much sadness in the woman and decided not to show her the bow and arrows right away. Instead, she held them behind her back as she chose her words carefully. "I've never eaten those before. Are they good?"

Buffalo Calf nodded. "My children would love them."

Ah-kah's eyes grew wide. "I did not know you have children."

Buffalo Calf looked up from her work. Ah-kah saw tears in her eyes. "Two. They are babies. The army would not let me bring them here. They said no children are allowed at the fort. But they allowed you to come. I do not understand why my children could not come too."

Ah-kah did not understand either, and she felt sorry for Buffalo Calf. She watched quietly as the warrior woman wiped away tears with the back of her hand. Then Buffalo Calf took a deep breath and used the open end of a glass to cut out circles in the dough.

"You are good with your hands," said Ah-kah. "I bet you can make anything."

Buffalo Calf sighed as she delicately peeled the round circles off the table and put them on a metal sheet.

Ah-kah asked the next question quietly. "Do you know how to fix feathers on arrows?"

"Of course," said Buffalo Calf, who went on to describe how to cut a long feather into thirds and then slice each third again straight down the quill. "Each arrow gets three halves of the feather."

"How do you keep them on the arrow?"

Buffalo Calf allowed herself a slight smile. "I chew dry deer muscle until it's sticky and tie them on tightly with that at the bottom and the top of the feathers. But you can use thread. Just don't use a lot or it will make the arrow too heavy. Then I glue the spines of the feathers to the arrow."

Ah-kah nodded. She was eager to stick the feathers on the arrows but didn't want to be rude by leaving too quickly.

Buffalo Calf put the cookies in the oven. When she turned back around she looked at Ah-kah quizzically. "Why are you asking about arrows?"

It was only then that the girl held up her bow and sharpened reeds. "Black Horse is going to teach me how to shoot."

Buffalo Calf stared at the bow and arrows for a long moment. She spoke quietly. "I was forced to learn how to use a bow and arrow when I was not much older than you." She looked so sad, Ah-kah thought Buffalo Calf was going to weep again.

She thanked her politely and quickly made her way to her family's room, where she found some thread. She had no glue but figured she could add that later. This would be enough to get started.

Chapter 8

Callie, June 12, 1875

Ben knocked on the screen door promptly at half past seven. I let James answer it and Ben stepped inside. My little brother wanted to tag along for a sweet cream soda at Hamblen's in the worst way. He asked Ben if he could join us, but Ben plainly told him no.

I pretended to ignore them both and busied myself in front of the hall mirror, arranging my hair under a straw bonnet. I could see James' reflection in the mirror. He was not happy to be told no and stomped outside to sit on the front porch.

Both Ben and I pretended we didn't see him as we hurried down the steps to Charlotte Street, one of the original streets laid out by the Spanish long ago. It was so narrow I'd caught tourists walking by our house with their arms fully extended, trying to touch both sides of the street at the same time.

When we got to Hamblen's we ordered two sweet cream sodas and settled in at a small table to wait for Mr. Hamblen's delicious concoction of ginger ale topped with a large dollop of ice cream.

"So, what's this idea you have for me?" I asked, leaning toward Ben, my forearms on the table. He smiled, and I enjoyed watching the corners of his eyes crinkle at their edges.

"The hotel addition is all but done," he said.

I nodded. Ben was a clerk at the St. Augustine Hotel, the most popular hotel in town. It was owned by Lieutenant Vaill, who'd been part of the Northern Navy during the War Between the States. He moved to St. Augustine after the war ended.

"These Natives are proving good for the tourist business. Bookings are way up. Travelers from all over the country want to come here to see them before they vanish from this earth."

I rolled my eyes, thinking of those ragtag men at the fort.

Ben shook his head in amazement. "I suggested to Lieutenant Vaill we make a special menu cover for the hotel's grand re-opening, and he agreed. He wants you to paint it!"

I grinned eagerly. "Oh Ben! That's wonderful!"

"He's going to pay you too!"

I hugged my hands to my chest. "This will be my first commission as a painter!"

Ben looked pleased. "He wants you to paint something that reflects the Natives' experience here, given that they're so popular with the tourists."

I suddenly felt less excited and was about to express my displeasure at Lieutenant Vaill's choice of subject matter when Mr. Hamblen brought our sodas and two spoons to the table. Ben reached into his pocket to pay, but Mr. Hamblen refused to take Ben's money. Instead he looked at me.

"I think it's wonderful that you're helping the Natives with the art classes, Miss Crump. My wife is teaching them to read, you know. We support what Lieutenant Pratt is trying to do. The sodas are on me."

A smile froze on my face. How could I accept Mr. Hamblen's generosity knowing I'd never teach at the fort again?

Ben, however, thanked Mr. Hamblen profusely and Mr. Hamblen returned to work.

I was no longer hungry. "I hate teaching the captives," I hissed.

Ben calmly spooned some ice cream into his mouth and raised his eyebrows in question.

"They don't even understand what I'm saying." I dug my spoon into my soda and angrily stirred it around. "How am I supposed to teach them anything when they don't speak English?"

"Isn't that the point?" Ben asked. "To teach them how to understand you?" He enjoyed more of his ice cream.

"One student is so angry he won't even look at me." And then I remembered something. "His name is White Horse. Have you heard of him? Do you know why he's here?"

Ben swallowed hard and sat up straighter. "I read about him. The papers say he killed cattlemen and stole cattle along the Chisholm Trail in North Texas and the Oklahoma Territory. He took a Texas farmer's wife hostage and their five children too. The army paid a big ransom to get them all back."

I shook my head, incredulous. "And why am I trying to teach him art of all things?"

"You're teaching him new ways, Callie. Isn't that what Lieutenant Pratt wants to do?"

I shook my head, recalling White Horse's simmering rage. "I'm not sure it's possible."

"What about your other students?"

I had to admit they were more receptive to my classwork.

"Well that's encouraging," Ben said. "And maybe White

Horse will come around. You've only had one class with him."

Ben was right. He was always right. Yet, the more sensible he sounded, the more selfish and miserable I became. "But I don't want to teach art, I want to make art," I cried.

Ben swallowed the last spoonful of his soda. "No one's stopping you. You have the menu covers . . . and art school in Philadelphia. Are you still planning to apply?"

I was surprised Ben mentioned Philadelphia. We didn't talk about it much, but since he brought it up, I blurted out another thing that had been on my mind of late. "Do you think I should go to Philadelphia?"

Ben chose his words carefully. "If it's your dream, yes, I think you should go. But not if it's someone else's dream for you."

I crossed my arms and sat back in my chair. Ben was referring to my mother, of course. It was her dream for me to go to Philadelphia for art school, but it was my dream too, or at least I thought it was.

I felt so confused. Ben, meanwhile, pointed to my sweet cream soda, a mischievous grin crossing his face. "Are you going to eat that?"

The moment for serious discussion had passed. I smiled and slid my glass across the table to Ben, fully knowing I'd return to the fort to teach again just as Ben had so calmly suggested.

Chapter 9

Ah-kah, August 25, 1875

Black Horse set down a burlap sack stuffed with straw in the fort's courtyard not far from his daughter. He made Ah-kah stand partly sideways to the sack, her feet shoulder-distance apart. Peonte watched quietly from the shade.

Black Horse showed Ah-kah again how to pull back the bow cord using just the tips of her first three fingers. And then he told her to let go of the bowstring.

Ah-kah's arrow sailed through the air and landed in the ground well beyond the sack. Her next arrow sailed wildly to the right. But she did not stop practicing until the tips of her fingers were red and nearly raw.

She was still practicing in just this fashion several days later when two Pale Face visitors, a man and woman touring the fort with Lieutenant Pratt, stopped to watch her. Ah-kah took a quick look at the woman and almost dropped her arrow. She wore a black straw hat with an entire blackbird sitting squarely on top of it. Ah-kah thought it utterly beautiful.

She tried to ignore the woman and her hat and concentrate on shooting. Her next arrow landed squarely in the sack, and the woman clapped approvingly. Ah-kah allowed herself a small smile, but found her eyes pulled to the bird, which, though dead, was now bobbing its head gently up and down on the lady's head.

The woman grabbed Lieutenant Pratt's forearm. "My son would love that bow and arrow set. Do you think the girl would sell it?"

Lieutenant Pratt, ever polite, smiled at the lady. "Let me get the translator. He will ask her."

Ah-kah watched the lieutenant walk away and return with Dick, who explained in Comanche that the woman wanted to buy her bow and arrows. Ah-kah hardly heard him. "Is that a real bird on her head?" she asked.

Dick looked at the woman's hat and suppressed a smile. "Yes," he replied. "The bird is stuffed. It's made to move with wires inside. Pale Face women think it very pretty."

Ah-kah thought it so very pretty as well. And she had questions, so many questions. The bird was stuffed? And made to move with wires? Did the woman make it? Could she make her one?

Dick, meanwhile, repeated the woman's request. "She wants to know if you will sell your bow and arrows."

Ah-kah swallowed hard. "Do you think she'd trade my bow and arrows for her hat?"

Dick translated Ah-kah's request. The woman patted her hat, smiled, and said something in English. Dick translated. "She says it is a new hat and she does not want to sell it. But she will give you one dollar and fifty cents for your bow and arrows."

Ah-kah's eyes popped. Once when there was no food back in Oklahoma, her father sold an entire buffalo robe that represented days and days of work for one dollar and fifty cents. Of course she would sell her bow and arrows for that same price.

Ah-kah eagerly handed the bow and arrows to the woman. The man who'd stood quietly at the woman's side throughout the encounter handed Ah-kah one dollar and fifty cents.

"Thank you," the woman said.

"Ajo," Ah-kah replied, taking a last look at the bird hat as the woman walked away.

She ran to find her mother and father sitting in the shade and handed them the money. Peonte, shocked to see the cash, made her tell the story of the woman with the bird hat, not once, but twice. The second time she told it, Black Horse paced back and forth in front of them, excited.

"I want to make more bows and arrows, Father," Ah-kah said. "The Pale Face will buy them. I want to send my money back to Kaku so she can buy food."

"We must all make them," said Black Horse. "The other tribes too. We can all send money back to Fort Sill."

Black Horse stopped pacing. "The chiefs must council with Lieutenant Pratt." He immediately left to round up the other chiefs and find the lieutenant.

As he hurried off, Ah-kah saw the same fat animal—the one she'd seen months before in the narrow corridor of the fort near the prison room. This time the animal darted across the courtyard. Dick had told her it was a mouser—a cat whose job it was to catch mice inside the fort and kill them.

Ah-kah followed the cat into the room with the cross, which she now knew was where the Pale Face worshipped their

Great Spirit. She sat quietly on a bench, watching the cat while it cleaned itself. Suddenly it stood up, walked toward her, and rubbed up against her leg, purring loudly.

Ah-kah scratched the cat behind its ear, appreciating the fact that it was a hunter and a good one. She picked it up and held its warm body close while it purred some more. Ah-kah smiled. "I will call you Te-ne-qua," she said. "Because you like to sing a lot."

The meeting between the chiefs and Lieutenant Pratt yielded some interesting results. Ah-kah overheard the details later that afternoon when Black Horse relayed them to Peonte.

Black Horse told Lieutenant Pratt the men wanted to make bows and arrows and any other trinkets they could think of to sell to tourists. Black Horse said this was important because the men could send money back home to help their families. They could also use their money to buy or trade for things like pipe tobacco or food. This, Black Horse pointed out, would be good business for traders in St. Augustine too. Lieutenant Pratt welcomed these ideas.

In exchange, Lieutenant Pratt told the Chiefs he wanted the men to live and work like soldiers. That meant he wanted them to have actual soldier jobs. For instance, Boy Hunting would become the quartermaster, in charge of making sure the Natives had the proper Pale Face clothing and supplies. White Horse was to be a sergeant, in charge of making sure the men did what they were supposed to do as soldiers. And Black Horse and other chiefs, including the Kiowa chief Lone Wolf and the Cheyenne chief Medicine Water were to council with Lieutenant Pratt on a regular basis to plan for the future, talk over problems, and find solutions.

Black Horse and the chiefs agreed to these requests.

They asked for knives to help the men make their trinkets and especially to cut notches in the tourists' bows and arrows. Lieutenant Pratt did not like this idea, but Black Horse pressed for this concession.

In the end, Lieutenant Pratt allowed the men one small penknife barely suitable for cutting notches in mulberry branches and reeds. Black Horse was to be in charge of it.

Lieutenant Pratt told the chiefs he'd gotten a request from a group of Pale Face women who lived in a place called Ohio. They wanted to come to St. Augustine so the Natives could give them archery lessons. Black Horse and the chiefs agreed, but said any Native who taught these lessons should be paid 50 cents per student per lesson. Lieutenant Pratt said he would tell this to the women in Ohio.

When Black Horse told Peonte all the news, she did not seem very pleased. She only wanted to know one thing.

"Did Lieutenant Pratt say how long we must stay here?" Peonte asked. Black Horse shook his head sadly. There had been no talk of that. Ah-kah sighed along with her mother.

She longed for cold nights. She longed to sleep in a teepee covered with soft furs. She longed to pick the sweet strawberries that carpeted the prairie in the spring. And most of all, she longed for the knot she felt deep in her stomach to go away. She knew this would only happen when her family was free again, and it made her angry that Lieutenant Pratt would not tell the prisoners how long they were to be held prisoner at the fort. A year? Two years? Forever?

To make matters worse, an old Pale Face woman had begun grabbing Ah-kah's hand every morning and taking her to the worship room for something called "lessons." The woman's name was Mrs. Mather. She reminded Ah-kah of a goat because she wore her hair in two small buns that stuck out like horns on either side of her head. She was teaching Ah-kah the Pale Face letters and their corresponding sounds used for reading and writing words. Ah-kah did not see the point in learning these things. She could not imagine ever using them once she returned home.

Mrs. Mather also forced her to speak English. Ah-kah thought Mrs. Mather should be made to learn Comanche.

One morning, Mrs. Mather decided to teach Ah-kah the English words for different parts of the body.

She tapped her ear. "Ear," Mrs. Mather said. Ah-kah dutifully repeated it. This went on for a while, with Mrs. Mather giving her the words for hand, foot, arm, and leg. Then Mrs. Mather tapped a tooth with her finger and said the word, "Tooth."

Ah-kah repeated it.

Then Mrs. Mather said the word "teeth" and to Ah-kah's dismay she took all her teeth out of her mouth! Ah-kah was horrified. She ran out of the classroom and across the court-yard, with Mrs. Mather's laughter echoing in her ears. She darted into an empty room and looked around for a hiding spot. Ah-kah noticed several cannons piled high in a corner. She lay down between the wall and the cannons and tried to get the disgusting picture of Mrs. Mather's tooth or teeth— she wasn't sure which—out of her head.

Ah-kah must have dozed off because when she awoke there were people about. She peered out between the cannons at White Horse and Boy Hunting, and the Cheyenne named Making Medicine. The Pale Face girl with hair the color of the sun, the one Ah-kah had seen painting outside the fort shortly after she arrived, was also there. So was the nice soldier named Falloon.

A large owl sat stiffly atop a barrel in the room. Ah-kah froze. It was extremely bad medicine to see an owl during the daytime. It meant death was coming sure as winter turns to spring.

The Pale Face girl was trying to get the men to sit down on the bench, but Ah-kah knew they would never do that because they'd have to walk past the owl to get there. Instead they crowded around the doorway.

Ah-kah considered running out of the room herself, but she did not want to pass by the owl either. However, if it hooted, she would have no choice. She would have to run. An owl's hoot was a very bad omen, not something anyone wanted to hear. Ah-kah held her breath, poised to bolt out the door if necessary.

Falloon said something to the painting teacher who now looked very confused. Just then Lieutenant Pratt marched into the room. Falloon gave a hand signal to the lieutenant, the same one Ah-kah always saw the soldiers give their chief. Lieutenant Pratt returned the signal and handed the girl a package.

The girl thanked him. Ah-kah knew the words for "thank you" in English. Then the three held a conversation she could not understand at all. It ended with Lieutenant Pratt picking up the owl and carrying it out the door. The Natives scattered when they saw the owl coming, but once it was gone, the men returned to the room and sat on the bench. Ah-kah relaxed as the Pale Face girl opened the lieutenant's package and handed each man a book, similar to the kind she'd seen the Pale Face write in before. The girl gave them each a set of colored pencils to go along with their books. How Ah-kah longed for pencils and a book just like the men now held!

The Pale Face girl instructed the men to open their books.

She sat before them so they could watch her draw. It looked to Ah-kah like the girl was drawing her very own hand while at the same time showing the men how to draw their hand as well.

Ah-kah was jealous. While she was with Mrs. Mather struggling to learn strange letters and sounds, these men got to learn drawing and were given their very own colored pencils and books to draw in. It was not fair!

Once the class ended and everyone left, Ah-kah waited a few moments and slipped out. She walked toward her tent but stopped short when she saw Mrs. Mather talking to Peonte and Black Horse. Dick was there too, translating. Ah-kah knew they were talking about her. She quickly climbed the stairs to the ramparts.

Black Horse had been clear since they'd arrived at the fort: He wanted his daughter to learn English. He would not be happy to learn she ran out of her lesson. Ah-kah knew she'd hear from her parents soon enough.

Chapter 10

Callie, September 15, 1875

I longed to create the most beautiful menu covers St. Augustine had ever seen. But given that my menu cover needed to showcase the Natives and their experience in our antique town, I had no idea what to paint.

A sunrise or sunset with cabbage palms in the foreground would have been lovely. Tourists adored our palm trees, many having never seen one until their visit here.

Or perhaps an orange tree would make a pleasing composition. Tourists loved the fresh orange juice they drank every morning made from oranges plucked from trees just outside their hotel rooms.

I even thought about painting Charlotte Street, the street where I lived. The purple bougainvillea would soon be in full bloom, and tourists always remarked that they'd never seen such an abundance of beautiful flowers as we enjoyed here in St. Augustine.

But Ben was clear: Lieutenant Vaill only wanted "the Native experience." Did that mean Natives in chains and shackles? Natives dressed like army soldiers making bows and arrows to sell to tourists? These hardly seemed like appetite-inducing covers for a menu.

Then one evening, as I prepared for bed, I glanced out my bedroom window and saw several thin lines of smoke coming from atop the fort. I stopped brushing my hair and pulled back the lace curtains to get a better look. That's when I saw the faint outline of a half dozen or so teepees sitting atop the fort's ramparts, pointing skyward like small bleached pyramids. Shadows from small campfires flickered around the edges of the teepees. What in the world were they doing up there atop the fort?

Since I would get no answer until the morning I went to bed and awoke early. Indeed, the makeshift village of teepees was still pointing skyward from the fort's ramparts, a morning fog curling around the cone tops of each dwelling.

I pulled off my nightdress and pulled on my beige linen and went downstairs. Dominga was just adding wood to the stove to boil water for coffee. She knew nothing of the teepees, and so I determined I would go and find out. Just in case, I gathered my twin boxes of paint and paper, my easel, and a Mason jar full of water and walked up the bluff to the guard hut in the dawn's early light. A soldier on duty was eager to talk.

"The captives think the mold growing on the walls inside the fort is making them sick," he said. "They asked the lieutenant if they could move up to the gunneries where the air is fresh. He said yes, and I think they slept peacefully. I didn't hear a peep from any of them," he said, yawning. I thanked the guard and hurried back down to the bottom of the hill.

When I turned around I saw the most beautiful pink and

blue sky set against the fort's dark coquina walls. I quickly set up my easel and started to sketch, my graphite scratching noisily as I worked to record the scene. When I had enough of an outline, I opened my paint box and applied a thin wash of pink to the sky and another of light blue. The sky created a feeling of hope in the picture, which I found appropriate given what Lieutenant Pratt was trying to do with the Natives.

I then selected the shell containing Payne's grey, knowing I could paint much of the fort in variant shades of my favorite trusty color. I painted the teepees last, using a thin brush and my shell containing marine blue. I knew the blue would contrast nicely with the other colors in the painting.

When I stepped back to look at what I'd done, I realized I'd missed something important: the American flag. Father had been a surgeon in the Northern Army during the War Between the States and had done his part to keep the Union together. I felt great love for this flag.

Using Alizarin scarlet and Prussian blue, I allowed myself to paint an American flag atop the ramparts, even though it was not atop the ramparts at all, but was actually flying from a pole not far from the guard hut. Still, I enjoyed the contrast of the flag flying beside the Natives' teepees, although I knew the Natives would not have wanted it there.

Pleased with the results, I headed home to find James hunched over the kitchen table, stuffing one of Dominga's just-baked cinnamon buns into his mouth.

"If Queen Victoria saw you eating like that, James, you'd be sent to the Tower of London." He ignored me and blissfully stuffed another large piece of cinnamon bun into his mouth. I sighed. It was not easy being a mother to this motherless child. Dominga poured a cup of coffee for me and changed the topic.

"What did you paint?"

"The captives set up teepees atop the ramparts at the fort. I think it will make a good menu cover." Dominga nodded. She knew of my struggle to find an appropriate scene for the hotel's grand re-opening.

"There's teepees at the fort?" James asked, displaying partially chewed food in his mouth.

I held my hand out to shield my eyes from his open mouth.

"That's disgusting!" James closed his mouth and chewed delicately, waiting for me to answer his question.

"Yes, there are teepees at the fort," I sighed. "The Natives want to sleep outside. They fear the mold at the fort is making them sick."

James slipped out of his chair. I knew where he was going and I tried to stop him. "Visiting hours at the fort start at three. We need to practice your multiplication tables now."

But James would have none of that. He disappeared out the kitchen door. I looked at Dominga. She shook her head. James was too wild for his own good.

Chapter 11

Ah-kah, September 24, 1875

For Ah-kah, life at the fort brought many changes. For instance, she no longer wore moccasins or her buckskin dress. It was just too hot. Instead she often went barefoot and wore either a red-checked or blue-checked gingham dress that Mrs. Mather had given her. The dresses once belonged to someone much larger than Ah-kah, but she wore them anyway despite their size, thankful for their comfort.

Ah-kah couldn't help but notice that Dick was dressing differently too. Since he was not required to wear an army uniform like rest of the men, he now wore pants the same color as deerskin, but made of cloth, along with a white shirt and black string tied around his neck. He shaved his hair up the sides just like the Pale Face and grew a mustache.

Sometimes Dick went to town and didn't come back by sundown. Peonte thought he had a girlfriend. Dick's absence was a problem for everyone because Dick was the most reliable translator there was at the fort. And when Dick was gone, no one collected reeds and branches, either.

This changed one afternoon when Black Horse needed more materials for bows and arrows. More tourists were coming to the fort every day to see the Natives, and the bows and arrows were selling well. There was talk of an archery tournament in the future, perhaps between tribes, something that would attract an even larger number of tourists. Black Horse wanted to have plenty of bows and arrows ready to sell.

"Do you think you can collect some reeds and branches without Dick?" Black Horse asked one buttery morning so hot Ah-kah thought she might melt. Summer lasted so long here in Florida. She longed for cooler weather.

Still, Black Horse had never before asked her to do something so important, and Ah-kah was thrilled. She remembered the promise she'd made to Dick not to leave the fort alone, but she was not about to mention it to her father, not now.

Ah-kah soon found herself headed out of the fort with Lieutenant Pratt's penknife tucked in her pocket. Black Horse watched from the ramparts as she climbed high into the mulberry tree at the base of the bluff. It wasn't easy to cut branches with the penknife, but she managed to get what she needed and drag the branches back to the fort.

Next, Ah-kah headed out to cut reeds. This time, she needed to go a lot farther, to an area where Black Horse could not keep his eye on her.

"Come right back," he said, looking her straight in the eye. "Please be careful."

Ah-kah nodded, and was soon walking atop the two-foot wide seawall. She passed a big steamboat docked to her left, its crew unloading boxes. Wagons and carriages passed by on her right. There were men and women on horseback dressed in fancy riding clothes, and people on the street walking barefoot, just like she was. Everyone seemed very busy.

Ah-kah soon came to the end of the seawall and the town. She jumped off the wall to the edge of the marsh, the brown muck squishing between her toes. Ah-kah began cutting reeds, careful not to cut more of the thick grass than she could carry. While she was bent over she noticed something round and flat and brown laying in the muck. It looked like a small turtle shell except that it's surface was smooth. Ah-kah poked it with a reed. When it did not move, she picked it up, noticing how thick and heavy it felt. She slipped it into her pocket to examine later.

Ah-kah soon had plenty of reeds and climbed back onto the seawall to return to the fort. Suddenly, something whizzed by her head and landed *plunk* in the water to her right. She turned to see the same two boys, Bumpy Nose and Spotted Face, who'd bothered her before. The bigger boy was about to throw an oyster shell at her.

"This is for you, Long Tail," he yelled.

Ah-kah turned and ran just as the shell hit her thigh. The boys threw more shells and yelled things she did not understand. Something hit her squarely in the back. It took her breath away. She found she couldn't run as fast as she wanted to run. Still, Ah-kah refused to let herself walk until she got to a busier part of town. She felt great relief when she finally reached to the fort. Black Horse was waiting for her.

Ah-kah tried not to look as shaken as she felt. "Everything go okay?" Black Horse asked, examining her closely.

Ah-kah nodded and transferred the reeds to his eager arms. She could not tell him about the boys. If she did, they'd never allow her to leave the fort again. And then who would collect reeds and branches to make into the bows and arrows to sell to tourists? Much of that money was sent back home. Ah-kah had seen the letters from her people at Fort Sill. The money the men were sending back home had become very important to Kaku and everyone else. She could not let anything happen to interrupt that process.

Ah-kah made her way to her tent and plopped down on her blanket. She breathed deeply, and looked at her thigh. A bruise was already beginning to form.

Tenequa padded into the tent and sat beside her. He purred and demanded to be scratched. Ah-kah's eyes watered as she pulled the cat toward her, squeezing her eyes shut. Why were those boys so mean to her? The older boys back home were not like that. Were all Pale Face boys this mean?

Ah-kah tried to cuddle with her cat, but a large lump in her pocket smashed against her side and made that difficult. She remembered the brown thing she'd found in the marsh and pulled it from her pocket. Ah-kah looked at it closely and decided it must be some kind of seedpod. She would ask Mrs. Mather to tell her the proper name for it.

As she studied the seedpod, Ah-kah had an idea. She'd been looking for something else to make beside bows and arrows since the men had all but taken over that work. Ah-kah would paint this seedpod and perhaps another Pale Face lady with a bird hat on top of her head would buy it.

Ah-kah felt herself relax as she closed her eyes. She hugged Tenequa. The cat purred warmly as Ah-kah forced the mean boys from her head replacing them with pictures of beautifully painted seedpods.

Chapter 12

Callie, September 27, 1875

My arms were full as I trudged up the hill for art class. I carried an old paintbrush, one I didn't use much anymore, and a set of paints. I'd brought the four primary colors in four different oyster shells since Mrs. Mather had asked me to bring painting supplies for the Comanche girl, Ah-kah. The girl wanted to paint sea beans, of all things.

I also carried colored pencils, a sketchpad, and a large and very heavy book by S. Sidney called *Illustrated Book of the Horse*. Father had bought me this detailed volume several years earlier to help me learn to draw animals. Between the pages of S. Sidney's book were color lithographs of all kinds of horses. I thought the Natives would enjoy looking at the pictures.

When I got to class I was surprised to see a new student, the Cheyenne woman known as Buffalo Calf, come into the classroom with a new ledger book. She wore her hair in two thin braids and seemed a gentle soul. I had to remind myself she was a warrior woman for her tribe and a murderess.

Falloon explained that Lieutenant Pratt sent Buffalo Calf to class because he thought art lessons would do her a "world of good."

"Otherwise," he continued, "she's not doing much with her days, Miss. The lieutenant hopes you can engage her."

I was honored that Lieutenant Pratt put so much stock in my abilities even though I truly did not know how to teach. I actually wished, however briefly, that I'd had some teacher training so that I could better engage my students.

Buffalo Calf and the men sat down on the bench. I smiled at her and she gave me a small smile in return.

I opened S. Sidney's book to a picture of a chestnut mare and held it up for the Natives to see. I quickly noticed they were, to a student, leaning forward to see the chestnut mare more closely.

I turned to a page containing a pair of brown and white Clydesdales. At this, White Horse stood up and stepped closer. He said something in his Native tongue and pointed to the horses' hooves, large and hairy. The other Natives, including Buffalo Calf, gathered round the book, which I laid atop the barrel. They all stared at the picture in wonder.

I stepped back to allow them to discover S. Sidney's book on their own. White Horse turned a few pages and found a tall white stallion. He stood transfixed to the page, stroking it with his fingers as if he were stroking the horse's neck.

I asked the Natives to draw their own pictures of a horse in their ledger books. White Horse, it seemed, could not take his eyes from the lithograph of the white stallion. He remained firmly rooted in front of the barrel staring at that picture.

I looked at Falloon, wondering what to do. He provided

his usual sage advice. "Might just want to leave him be, Miss," he said. I agreed.

Boy Hunting drew a lovely sketch of a Native wearing a feather headdress while sitting atop a gray spotted horse. He added colored pencil to it too.

Buffalo Calf sat on the bench and opened her ledger book to draw a picture of a teepee in a village. There was no horse in her sketch, but there was a mother and child standing beside the teepee holding hands. They looked happy.

It seemed these pictures were all quite telling of the state of my students' most private thoughts. If this were the case, then Making Medicine drew the most interesting sketch of all. He drew a picture of a group of Natives in their army garb sitting on benches in the chapel room. One Native stood in front of the rest with the cross in the background. He read from a black book that I took to be the Bible. I made a note to tell Mrs. Mather of Making Medicine's sketch. She would be quite pleased, as I knew that Mrs. Mather and her women were teaching the Natives about Jesus.

In my case, I opened my sketchbook and drew the chestnut mare I'd just seen in the book. I thought it would be lovely to ride such a fine horse while sitting sidesaddle and wearing an elaborate riding costume. I went on to fill in my sketch work with some colored pencils.

We all worked in companionable silence (except for White Horse, who did not work at all) until Falloon announced it was time to end our class. He ushered everyone out and I closed S. Sidney's *Illustrated Book of the Horse*, knowing we'd use it in class again someday.

When I left the fort, I decided to visit Ben at the St. Augustine Hotel. From the moment I stepped into its lobby, the hotel's improvements were apparent. A red circular sofa covered in silk fabric stood in the center of the lobby, replacing the hotel's old white wicker furniture. New potted palms stood sentry beside full-length windows. Gas lamps hung on the walls. Ben said there was a similar lamp in every room. Only the hotel's immense grand staircase, its balustrades carved from some exotic wood to resemble the thick twisted rope of a ship, appeared unchanged.

Ben smiled when he saw me. "Three more bookings today for November and December," he called across the lobby. "All to see the Natives."

"That's excellent!" I exclaimed, as I walked up to the front desk.

"Holy Moses," he added. "These Natives are great for business!"

I leaned against the front desk and surveyed the lobby. "It looks lovely in here. When do the guests begin arriving?"

"The toxophilites arrive in two weeks."

"Goodness, who are they?" I'd never heard that word before. Ben smiled. "They are the ladies from Ohio I told you about. Toxophilites are lovers of the bow. Fifteen of them. Lieutenant Pratt has arranged for archery lessons up at the fort. Oh, and Lieutenant Vaill sent your menu cover to the printer in Jacksonville."

I clapped my hands, thrilled at all his news.

"He wants more menu covers too. He said one every month during the season." Ben suddenly lowered his voice. "I told him that wouldn't be a problem. It's okay, isn't it?"

I frowned. "Do they all need to depict the Natives?"

Ben winked. "I give you creative license."

"Then I'm thrilled," I said, smiling.

Just then the staccato sounds of hammer on nail suddenly filled the air. I looked at Ben questioningly.

M.C. Finotti

"The carpenters are putting the finishing touches on the cabinets for the porcelain tubs."

I sighed at the thought of such a marvelous innovation. Ben had told me that every room at the hotel would now have its own porcelain tub. Oh how I longed to bathe in one of these inventions. I'd seen pictures of them in magazine advertisements, which claimed the tub felt "as slippery as glass when filled with water." I longed to lie back and relax in one till my skin grew pink and wrinkled.

"Would you like to see one?" Ben asked.

I blushed, knowing it would be practically scandalous for me to view a tub with Ben at my side. As much as I wanted to see these bathing advancements, I found a quick excuse. "I've got new menu covers to paint!"

On my walk home I couldn't help but feel pleased. After all, I now had an ongoing commission to paint menu covers for Lieutenant Vaill. An interesting thought began to take shape in my mind, and maybe even in my heart. Perhaps I didn't need to go to Philadelphia for art school after all.

Chapter 13

Ah-kah, September 27–October 27, 1875

Mrs. Mather handed Ah-kah four small shells containing dried cakes of paint. She also handed her a paintbrush just like the one Ah-kah had seen the painting teacher use outside the fort shortly after she'd arrived.

Mrs. Mather smiled. "Now you can paint your sea bean," she said.

"Ajo," said Ah-kah, wide-eyed.

"Use your English," said Mrs. Mather, not unkindly.

"Thank you," said Ah-kah, too excited with the set of paints to feel bothered at Mrs. Mather's insistence that she speak English.

Mrs. Mather pointed to Ah-kah's sea bean. "You should polish it first."

Ah-kah frowned. Mrs. Mather realized the child didn't know what she meant. "Wait here," Mrs. Mather motioned with her hand, as she she marched off. She quickly returned with a small square of sandpaper. "Give me the sea bean." She held out her hand.

Ah-kah reluctantly turned over her sea bean and Mrs. Mather showed her how to lightly sand it to bring a shiny, brown luster to its surface. Ah-kah spent the entire day doing just that. Then she spent the next week carefully practicing how to paint delicate bows and arrows, colorful teepees and miniature horses on any surface she could find—the side of a barrel, the side of her teepee, even on a page of Black Horse's ledger book where he kept track of how much money each Native earned by making and selling bows and arrows.

She didn't even mind when Mrs. Mather insisted Ah-kah practice her letters. "I will write to Kaku," Ah-kah said. "But first there is someone else I will write to."

Mrs. Mather tilted her head to one side, waiting.

"I want to write to your Great Father in Washington."

Mrs. Mather thought a moment, as she tried to figure out what Ah-kah meant. And then it dawned on her. The girl wanted to write a letter to President Grant. "Excellent," Mrs Mather said. "I will see that it gets mailed to him once it is complete."

Ah-kah worked hard on this letter and found she only needed Mrs. Mather's help with some of the words. This is what she wrote:

Dear Mr. Grant,

When can we go home? I want to see my Kaku. Why can't we go home? My mother's name is Peonte. My father's name is Black Horse, Comanche Chief. My name is Ah-kah.

Thank you,

Ah-kah.

Ah-kah hoped she would get a reply, even though Mrs. Mather told her the Great Father was a very busy man and might not write back.

Ah-kah even dreamed of the letter she would receive, although one morning she awoke after a very different dream. She'd been chasing an eagle feather as it floated through the air. Ah-kah didn't know why she dreamed of such a thing, especially because only a man could earn an eagle feather for doing something very, very brave.

Still, Ah-kah rubbed the sleep from her eyes, grabbed her paintbrush and paints and crawled out of the teepee where she now slept atop the ramparts. She carefully painted an eagle feather on each side of her sea bean, and held the bean at arm's length to admire her work. Ah-kah hoped to sell the sea bean at an upcoming archery tournament. She smiled to herself thinking of the money she would send to Kaku and the licorice whips she would buy with what was left over from the sale.

By mid-October, Ah-kah found herself watching Making Medicine teach a group of fifteen Pale Face ladies the finer points of archery. She'd been watching every one of his classes because she wanted to improve her archery skills just as they did. Ah-kah quickly realized that the Pale Face women—who called themselves The Merry Maids of Marion, Ohio—were quite good at drawing a long bow at long-range targets some sixty yards away. But these women wanted to learn short-range archery, the kind Ah-kah was practicing, the kind Natives used to hunt small animals at close range with small bows.

After two weeks of daily lessons, all attended by Ah-kah, it was time for an archery competition between the Natives and the Merry Maids. The group's president, Alexandra Holmes Harding, was so sure one of her ladies would win this competition that she put up a fifteen-dollar prize that would go to the archer with the best record in both the long-range and short-range competitions. The tournament was to be held in the fort's courtyard.

On the afternoon of the long-awaited event, all the Natives and many of the townspeople gathered on the ramparts to wait for the competition to begin in the courtyard below.

Ah-kah laid her blanket out in front of her teepee. She placed her sea bean atop the blanket and sat down ready to entertain offers from prospective buyers. Beside her, Black Horse and some others sat on a blanket of their own ready to sell the piles of bows and arrows that were heaped beside them. Buffalo Calf was even there selling her molasses cookies.

Plenty of Pale Face walked by, but no one offered to buy Ah-kah's sea bean. This bothered her at first, but then she realized no one was buying the bows and arrows or the cookies, either. She decided sales of all trinkets and food would improve after the tournament. Thus, with the competition about to begin, she left her blanket and sea bean and sat down beside Peonte to watch the archers in the courtyard below.

Several bales of hay were stacked one atop the other at the far end of the courtyard. Pinned to the front of this stack was a bulls-eye target that had been painted on a piece of burlap.

The women lined up first. Each lifted a long bow to shoot three arrows at the target. Most of their arrows hit some portion of the bulls-eye, which Lieutenant Pratt dutifully recorded in a notebook. Only three of the Merry Maids, including Mrs. Harding, hit the bright yellow center of the bull's-eye to advance to the next round.

The Natives went next. White Horse hit the yellow center each time he drew his long bow, as did a Comanche named Red Antelope and a Kiowa named High Forehead. Making Medicine did not participate in the tournament. Ah-kah decided this must have been because he was the women's teacher.

After a break to move the targets forward, the short competition began with smaller bows and arrows. Mrs. Harding was the only Pale Face lady to hit the yellow bull's-eye each time. The crowd clapped politely. The only Native to hit the same target the same number of times was White Horse. The crowd clapped again and Ah-kah figured the competition would end in a tie.

But after a brief conversation between Lieutenant Pratt, Making Medicine and the two remaining contestants, the lieutenant stood in the middle of the courtyard and made an announcement. He held up a stuffed sack that reminded Ah-kah of the target her father had made for her when she first took up a bow and arrow.

"We shall have a tie-breaker round," Lieutenant Pratt called out. "Each contestant will get the chance to hit this target." He held up the sack and the crowd murmured its excitement. Lieutenant Pratt placed the sack on the ground not too far away.

Mrs. Harding shot first. She easily hit the sack. Her Merry Maids cheered.

White Horse shot next. He hit the sack too. The Cheyenne whooped loudly.

Lieutenant Pratt moved the target farther away. Again, both hit the target and again Lieutenant Pratt moved it farther away still. In fact, the third time it was so far out that Ah-kah wondered if the contestants should not change back to their long bows, but neither did.

Mrs. Harding lined up to shoot. She drew back her short bow and twang, let lose her bow cord. Her arrow sailed straight and strong, but landed short of the bag with a thud. The crowd gasped collectively.

Now White Horse stepped up confidently to the line. With refined and practiced movements, he drew back a mighty bow and aimed his arrow higher than Mrs. Harding had done. The arrow sailed through the air on its controlled flight and landed thump in the center of the sack. All the Natives cheered at such a display of skill. Ah-kah jumped up and down and hugged her father. Mrs. Harding, a noble loser, smiled and clapped for White Horse. She pulled a small velvet bag from her pocket and held it up for all to see.

"White Horse has won the purse," she announced, handing the velvet bag to the Cheyenne, who quietly accepted it, standing tall. Mrs. Harding continued. "I want you to know, White Horse, I look forward to another competition again next year." At this, White Horse grew very, very still. So did all the men. Ah-kah knew what they were thinking. Would they still be held prisoner at this fort one year from now? The excitement of White Horse's win vanished in that moment.

Ah-kah returned to her blanket hoping to sell her sea bean, but when she got there she was shocked to find the sea bean nowhere in sight. Ah-kah looked for it frantically. She shook out the blanket. She asked Black Horse if he knew where it went. But he simply shook his head. He was far too busy selling bows and arrows to help. Suddenly, Ah-kah heard a boy yell, "Throw it, James!"

She looked up to see Spotted Face across the rampart throwing her painted sea bean to Bumpy Nose. The two were playing a game of catch with the very sea bean she had painted and hoped to sell to a tourist! Ah-kah was furious. She walked over to the boy closest to her. "You stole that from me," she hissed.

Bumpy Nose looked at her and laughed. "I didn't steal anything. It was just sitting on a blanket. Someone left it." He threw the sea bean to Spotted Face at the precise moment that Ah-kah dove for it. Bumpy Nose stepped neatly aside and Ah-kah fell to the ground in front of him. Then Bumpy Nose pretended to trip over Ah-kah, kicking her in the process.

Ah-kah got to her feet, her hands balled into fists, prepared to kick the boy back. Just then the painting teacher intervened. "Willie and James, what are you boys doing?" she demanded, looking angrily at Bumpy Nose and then at Spotted Face.

"Playing catch," Spotted Face announced as his friend threw the sea bean toward him.

"That's my sea bean," Ah-kah said angrily, pointing to her trinket as it flew through the air far from her reach.

"Did you take this from her?" the painting teacher demanded, looking suspiciously at Spotted Face.

"We found it on a blanket, didn't we, Willie?" He heaved the sea bean back toward Bumpy Nose.

Bumpy Nose caught it. "We didn't take anything from anybody."

"Give it to the back her," said the painting teacher. The boys did nothing. "Now!"

Ah-kah could tell the boys did not like being told what to do. Bumpy Nose threw the sea bean toward his friend, using far more muscle than the throw required. The sea bean sailed over the wall of the fort, into the water. Ah-kah ran to the wall and looked over the edge. Her sea bean was nowhere in sight. She heard the painting teacher yell at Spotted Face. "James! I am going to speak to Father about you. Tonight!"

Ah-kah turned to see Spotted Face make an ugly face and run away with Bumpy Nose. The painting teacher approached her. "I am so sorry," she said. "My brother is awful. Mrs. Mather told me how hard you worked on that sea bean."

Ah-kah nodded.

"I know you were trying to sell it," she said. "I will give you some money."

Ah-kah shook her head sadly and walked away. The painting teacher called after her. "I have a sea bean at home. I will bring it to you."

But Ah-kah did not hear her. She crawled into her teepee, pulled the blanket over her head, and sank into the darkness.

Chapter 14

Callie, October 27–November 6, 1875

That evening at supper James eagerly recounted the archery tournament for Father in between pauses to slurp Dominga's peppery Minorcan clam chowder from his spoon.

As he prattled on, I felt sad. I had failed my brother in so many ways, not least of which was in teaching him how civilized people should eat their meals. Despite my best efforts, James' table manners were atrocious, and my father, who had perfect table manners, would not correct him. He believed James would eventually learn by example, a theory James continued to disprove.

"I don't know why that tourist thought she could best a Native in archery." *Slurp.* "Because of course she lost. We needed to put up someone better, *slurp,* for that tournament. Like that Negro man who's practically a Native himself. I bet he knows how to shoot an arrow." *Slurp.*

I held my tongue as long as I could. "Eat quietly, James."

Father gave me a warning look. He did not like bickering at the supper table. "Were you at the tournament, Callie?"

I put down my spoon. "I was." I eyed my brother, who also put down his spoon. "I caught James and Willie teasing Ah-kah, the Native girl at the fort."

James immediately jumped to his own defense. "We were not."

"You took her trinket and wouldn't give it back. And then Willie threw it into the water."

"We didn't know it was hers. It was just sitting on a blanket."

"It was a painted sea bean! Something like that doesn't just fall from the sky, James."

Dominga entered the dining room just then, forcing us to be silent. She carried a large blue and white soup tureen, one of Mother's special things. "Another bowl, Dr. Crump?"

"No thank you, Dominga. It's delicious, but I've had plenty."

I declined a second helping too, but James wanted more. Dominga carefully ladled the soup into his bowl and returned with the tureen to the kitchen. James began to eat and I waited for Father to say something about my brother's behavior at the fort.

Father cleared his throat. "James, you know I believe in assertiveness. It's an important trait for a successful man." James looked up from his soup bowl and nodded. We had both heard this lecture before. "But I cannot allow you to tease people," Father added.

"I didn't . . ." said James, trying to defend himself.

Father interrupted him. "Listen to me, please."

James stopped eating and looked solemnly at Father.

"I do not want to hear another story about you teasing anyone. Do you hear me? Simply stay away from that girl."

James hung his head. "Yes, Father."

I could not hold back any longer. "I do not believe that Willie is a good influence on James. I think it would be far better . . ."

"Enough!" Father stopped me mid-sentence. "James knows the right path to take no matter who his friends are."

Father looked pointedly at James, who at least seemed to be taking father's scolding to heart.

"This will be the end of it then," said Father. He folded his napkin and left the table.

I had hoped to find Ah-kah during my next visit to the fort and give her my sea bean. I was eager to see how she was doing. But I was not able to do so. That's because my next visit to the fort was equally as troubling as the one before, although in a far different way.

On this morning, I'd just read an article in *Scribner's Magazine* about a new French art movement called *en plein air*. The article explained how French artists were taking their canvases outdoors to paint in the natural light. Since Mother and I had always painted this way, I decided my class would too.

And so I led my tiny band of artists, and Falloon, up to the ramparts to paint *en plein air*. We opened our ledger books and had just settled in to sketch sailboats bobbing in the bay when Buffalo Calf jumped up and ran to the fort's wall. She pointed excitedly at the water below and began chanting in her Native tongue.

Her actions made Falloon and me nervous, as we saw nothing in the water that would agitate her so. Almost as suddenly as she began, Buffalo Calf stopped chanting and stood quietly staring at the water below. A pod of dolphins broke the water's surface and disappeared. I looked at Buffalo Calf. Tears streamed down her face and she began to tell a story, which Making Medicine translated, as best he could.

"Eleven winters ago," Buffalo Calf began, "my people decided to fight no more. We wanted to sleep in peace. And so we

M.C. Finotti

joined other Cheyenne led by Chief Black Kettle and walked to Fort Lyon in the southeast Colorado Territory. We planned to surrender.

"We set up camp on a wide sandy creek bed and our runners carried a white flag to tell the army at Fort Lyon why we had come. My mother was so happy. She hoped her grandchildren would go to school and learn to read. That night was very cold and we all slept like puppies underneath our buffalo robes."

Buffalo Calf wiped her eyes, never looking at Making Medicine or Falloon or me. She stared straight ahead at the water, lost in her story. I feared what she would say next.

"We woke at dawn to the thunder of horses' hooves. I looked out of the teepee to see hundreds of soldiers attacking us. One of the chiefs, White Antelope, stood before the soldiers with his arms folded so they could see he carried no weapon. He yelled, 'Soldiers no hurt me. Soldiers my friends,' but the soldiers killed him anyway.

"We were about to run out the back of the teepee when a soldier stormed in. My mother grabbed my grandfather's rifle but the soldier was too quick. He shot her in the forehead and then attacked me. I fought him hard. During the fight I grabbed my husband's knife and killed him.

"I snatched my children, one by the hand, the other in my arms, and we ran up the creek bed. We took nothing with us, not even our buffalo robes. Soldiers fired all around us. I saw some of the soldiers jump off their horses to kill wounded men with their knives." She sighed. "The water of the creek ran red."

At this memory Buffalo Calf stopped talking. She pinched the bridge of her nose with her thumb and forefinger and dropped her head. A loud sob escaped her throat.

"My son, whose hand I held, tripped and fell. I looked back

and called his name. He got up and ran toward me only to fall again, shot by a soldier's bullet.

"Bullets flew very close to me. One hit my baby in the head and killed her. It was only because of the Great Spirit that I too was not shot. I did not stop running until I saw some women from our tribe digging holes in the sand with their hands and hiding in the holes. I did the same. This is where I left my baby."

I was stunned to hear this story. Falloon, however, knew all about it. He whispered the details. "It was a terrible massacre. It happened during the War Between the States. The man who ordered it was Colonel John Chivington."

"Please tell me he was court-martialed."

"No, Miss. Some people in the Colorado Territory actually approved of what he'd done. But others, especially some of his men, did not. They reported him to Washington. Congress held hearings. Chivington's ambition was to become Colorado's first governor once it became a state, but the massacre ruined his career."

Making Medicine nodded toward Buffalo Calf. "This is why she became a warrior woman."

Suddenly, Buffalo Calf pointed to the water again as the pod of dolphins returned. They swam by the fort, their fins cresting the surface with ease. She smiled through her tears. Making Medicine translated.

"See the three dolphin-buffalo? She says they are messengers sent from her mother and children. Buffalo Calf says they came to tell her they are at peace. They are with the Great Spirit."

Later that night as I lay in bed I tried to push the horror of Colonel Chivington from my mind. I thought of Buffalo Calf and how she believed the dolphins had brought her a message from her loved ones. And I actually envied her. I wished they would bring me a message too, one from my mother.

M.C. Finotti

Chapter 15

Ah-kah, November 15, 1875

Ah-kah had no desire to leave the fort anymore. She wanted only to curl up on her side in her teepee with Tenequa, as the cat purred reassuringly against the curve of her body.

Peonte was sure her daughter was getting sick. She lit a stick of cedar, blew out the fire and waved the smoke over the girl's body, hoping to rid it of any ailments.

Dick tried to get Ah-kah to help him gather more bendable branches and tough reeds, but Ah-kah refused, saying she was too tired. Mrs. Mather asked Ah-kah to walk with her to town after class, but Ah-kah shook her had and said, "No thank you," in just the manner Mrs. Mather had taught her.

Only the art teacher, whom Ah-kah now called Callie, knew what had happened. Ah-kah realized Spotted Face was the teacher's brother and she knew Callie felt bad because he was so mean, so opposite from her. Callie offered to take her to Hamblen's and buy her some licorice whips, but Ah-kah did not feel like being pleasant and so she declined.

She asked Callie not to tell anyone how the boys had stolen her sea bean.

"Why?" Callie asked.

"Because my mother will learn of it and think them dangerous. She will make me stay by her side."

The art teacher pressed her hand to her heart. "Oh you poor thing," she said. "Father has told James in no uncertain terms not to tease you ever again. If he bothers you in the least you must let me know."

Ah-kah nodded. Still, she did not feel like her old self again until Black Horse insisted she go on a trip to see the Great Father of all Waters, the Atlantic Ocean. Black Horse said a change of scenery would do Ah-kah a world of good. And so on a blue-sky day, Lieutenant Pratt, Ah-kah, and some twenty prisoners and soldiers piled into two wide boats to row across the river from the fort to a tidal lagoon.

Once in the lagoon, Ah-kah noticed a disruption in the other rowboat, the one containing Lieutenant Pratt. A Cheyenne prisoner named Roman Nose pulled in his oar and pointed repeatedly at the water. The others in his boat moved to see what he was pointing at and nearly tipped over.

The men in Ah-kah's boat, eager to see what Roman Nose had seen, rowed over to join them. Ah-kah looked into the water to see three buffalo-sized gray and hairless creatures floating just below the water's surface. One of them looked up at Ah-kah with small beady eyes, unblinking. Ah-kah jumped back.

"Those are sea cows," Lieutenant Pratt called. "They won't hurt you." Ah-kah wasn't so sure.

The men beached their boats on the shores of the lagoon and Lieutenant Pratt led them across a wide and hilly expanse of sand to the beach. Ah-kah had never seen such a vast body of water. She rushed to the ocean's edge and immediately got her feet wet, enjoying the sensation of sinking in the sand each time the water receded. She looked down to see scores of tiny violet shells in the sand. They were so shiny and beautiful Ah-kah couldn't help but pick them up. She'd soon collected a pocketful.

Farther up the beach a group of Natives formed a chain, hand to hand, and ventured into the surf. The man at the far end of the chain jumped over the frothy waves, whooping with delight. Inevitably, he'd lose his footing, but the others held on tight until he stood up again, shaking his head to clear the seawater from his nose and eyes.

Ah-kah noticed Boy Hunting sketching something with a stick in the wide expanse of sand. She walked toward him and squatted down nearby to watch. He was so absorbed in his work that Ah-kah did not want to interrupt him.

Boy Hunting sketched a very large horse, then dropped to his knees and began shoving large heaps of sand into the center of his drawing to make the horse rise from the sand. He used brown plants that he found along the shoreline to make the horse's mane and tail. He then pulled a sea bean out of his pocket and used it to make the horse's eye.

Ah-kah jumped when she saw the sea bean. "Where did you find that?"

Boy Hunting looked up and blinked, disoriented for a second. He pointed toward the wide expanse of sand they walked across earlier. "Just up there."

Ah-kah soon found a half dozen sea beans, and many more types of shells. She also found several long gray feathers, which she collected to give to Peonte, who was saving them to make a headdress for Black Horse.

In the boat on the way back to the fort, her pockets bulging, Ah-kah thought about her treasures. It might be nice to tie some of the shells to the fringe of her old buckskin dress, she thought. They would make a lovely *tinkling* sound when she danced. She thought about gluing the tiny purple shells to a box as decoration. And she thought about polishing and painting all the sea beans she'd found. Ah-kah smiled to herself, realizing she was eager to get back to work making trinkets to sell to the tourists.

Chapter 16

Callie, December 5, 1875

B en read the letter as we enjoyed a sweet cream soda at
Hamblen's. It was such wonderful news, I asked him to
read it again. He smiled, theatrically cleared his throat, and read:
Dear Lieutenant Vaill,

Mr. Flower has not stopped talking about our recent trip
to St. Augustine. He is still telling our friends about his
encounter with the Native peoples at the fort, which brings
me to the reason for this letter.

I want to give him a copy of your menu cover, the one
of the fort with the teepees on the ramparts. It needs to be
suitable for framing as I plan to hang it in his office.

Would it be possible for your painter to re-create this for me?
I eagerly await your reply.
Sincerely,
Mrs. Sarah Flower, Watertown, New York

I clapped my hands and leaned past my sweet cream soda,
grinning from ear to ear. I had a hundred questions. "How big

do you think I should paint it?"

Ben answered thoughtfully. "Not too large. It must still be sent to New York."

"Perhaps I should paint the fort at a different time of day . . . a different light?"

Ben shook his head as he swallowed a spoonful of his foamy concoction. "Mrs. Flower said she wanted a copy of the menu cover. Nothing new."

I dug my spoon into my glass and took a bite. "How soon do you think it should be done?"

"Soon," Ben said. "Don't wait. You must strike while the iron is hot."

Suddenly worried, I sat back and frowned. "How much should I charge?"

Ben stopped his spoon in midair. He sat up taller. "Twenty dollars. And that could include shipping."

My eyes grew big as saucers. "Really?"

Ben nodded. "I remember this couple. They can afford it."

We walked home from Hamblen's atop the sea wall, enjoying the mild December evening. I told him about my idea for the menu cover for the hotel's New Year Celebration. "I'm going to paint the comedy and tragedy masks. That's perfect, don't you think?"

Ben answered by wiggling his hand into mine. I lost my breath for a second. He'd never held my hand before and I hoped, given the darkness, he couldn't see me blush.

We walked quietly after that and I made sure to pull my hand away before we got too close to home. I didn't want Father to see us. If he had, I feared the next time I left the house with Ben we'd be accompanied by a chaperone.

Chapter 17

Ah-kah, December 10, 1875

Ah-kah wore out the small square of sandpaper Mrs. Mather had given her. She got another piece from Falloon and used it to coax the shine out of each of her sea beans. Once finished, Ah-kah carefully painted designs on each one: a horse, a buffalo, a bow and arrow, a teepee, even a picture of Tenequa curled up in a ball on Peonte's colorful blanket.

There was to be a powwow at the fort on a Sunday afternoon in several weeks and Ah-kah planned to display her trinkets in hopes of selling them. The powwow was a big deal. Lieutenant Pratt had agreed to allow a photographer to be there so tourists could pose for pictures with Black Horse, or Lone Wolf, or another chief for fifty cents. The chiefs and the photographer would split the proceeds fifty-fifty.

Peonte was almost finished with the headdress Black Horse would wear to the powwow. Some of the men were planning a dance they would perform for the tourists. Black Horse had even asked Lieutenant Pratt if a buffalo could be shipped to St. Augustine from the Oklahoma Territory so the Natives could conduct a buffalo hunt. But Lieutenant Pratt said no, fearing a buffalo was just too much.

Ah-kah wanted to decorate a cigar box Dick had given her with the small violet shells she found on the beach. She was sure it would fetch a high price at the powwow, but she needed glue. Mrs. Mather didn't have any. She suggested Ah-kah ask Callie for some.

Ah-kah caught up with Callie after art class one morning. "Do you have some glue? I need to glue shells to a box."

"Yes, I do!" said Callie, smiling. Callie was happy to see the girl busy again. "In fact, why don't you bring your shells to my house and we could work on your box together."

Ah-kah had no desire to go to the home of Spotted Face. Still, she really wanted the glue. And she always wondered what life was like inside one of those stiff boxes the Pale Face called home. What did it look like inside? What did it smell like? She was certain it would not be as peaceful, nor smell as sweet, as her teepee back home. Perhaps she could go and not stay too long.

"I must ask my mother," she replied.

The art teacher nodded. "Of course."

Ah-kah found Peonte poking a pile of turkey, goose, and seagull feathers into a 4-inch-wide band of soft rawhide for Black Horse's headdress. Back home, her father's headdress was always made of eagle feathers, and the fact that this one would be far different made Ah-kah sad. She didn't want her mother to know that though. Peonte was working hard to make this headdress as beautiful as possible.

Peonte said she could not go inside the Pale Face teacher's home, although she could walk there to borrow the glue and come right back. That was fine with Ah-kah, who soon found herself peering through a doorway into the art teacher's warm and inviting kitchen. It looked about the same as the kitchen at the fort, with a big black iron box that Ah-kah knew was called a stove. It also smelled sweet and wonderful. Ah-kah had never smelled anything quite like it before.

Callie went upstairs to get some glue, while a woman working at the stove offered Ah-kah a light brown cookie with bits of sugar on top. Ah-kah thought this cookie quite strange. It wasn't round like the ones Buffalo Calf made. This one was shaped like a little person. Ah-kah frowned and held it out, examining it.

The woman laughed. "It's a gingerbread man. Eat it. It's good."

Ah-kah smiled uncertainly and took a small bite, just to be polite. The cookie was tasty, she had to admit. The cookie was gone by the time Callie returned with the small pot of glue.

"Here you go," Callie said, handing her the pot.

"Ajo."

Callie smiled. "Ajo."

Ah-kah turned to leave and Dominga asked her to wait.

She handed the girl a small stack of her cookies wrapped in a napkin. "Take these home with you," she said, smiling.

Ah-kah almost told the woman the fort was not her home, but she did not want to seem rude. She thanked them both and headed through the big backyard toward the gate.

As she approached the privy, she heard a familiar voice. Ah-kah froze. She could not see who was speaking—the speaker was standing behind the privy, but she knew that voice all too well.

"Stand with your feet apart. Like this," Bumpy Nose said. "And then drop the knife. Like this."

Ah-kah heard a *thud*. "The one who sticks the knife into the ground closest to their feet wins."

"What if I hit my foot?" another voice grumbled. Ah-kah knew that voice too. It was Spotted Face.

"Then you automatically lose. It's called mumblety-peg. You want to play?"

Ah-kah crept to the edge of the privy and peered around the corner. She thought Spotted Face did not look too enthusiastic about this game, but he nodded, signaling he was ready to try.

Bumpy Nose went first. Standing tall and looking down at scuffed leather shoes, he dropped his knife between his feet. It stuck in the ground. Spotted Face went next. His knife stuck in the ground too.

"Now we go a little closer together," Bumpy Nose said, as he moved his feet about three inches apart. He looked down, took aim, and dropped his knife between his feet. *Thud.*

Spotted Face did the same. Ah-kah had never seen such a stupid game. The boys back home never played this. They knew better. These boys were wearing leather shoes, but still the knife could go right through them.

Ah-kah dared not breathe as Bumpy Nose called for the boys to move their feet even closer, about an inch apart. He dropped his knife. It stuck in the ground between his feet.

Spotted Face did not look like he wanted to play anymore, but he took a deep breath and dropped his knife, hoping it would land in the small space between his shoes.

"Owwwww!" he yelled.

Ah-kah did not wait to see any more. She ran out of the backyard with those screams echoing in her ears and the image of the knife sticking in the top of Spotted Face's foot. She didn't stop until she was back at the fort, safely beside Peonte, where she shared the cookies with her mother.

Chapter 18

Callie, December 26, 1875

I spent the morning after Christmas in bed enjoying the soothing scent of rosemary leaves Dominga had sewn into my mattress for my Christmas gift. I read my favorite book, *Little Women,* by Louisa May Alcott even though I'd already read it twice before. I especially liked the part when Jo said she wanted to do something with her writing talent. The line goes like this: "I want to do something splendid before I go into my castle—something heroic, or wonderful—that won't be forgotten after I'm dead."

I knew that feeling. I wanted to do something splendid with my painting. Did that mean Philadelphia? Or New York? Or becoming a famous artist in St. Augustine? I simply wasn't sure.

But Jo never realized her dream. She gave up writing to marry Professor Bhaer. I was beginning to understand that too. Was it not a triumph to marry a good person like Professor Bhaer or even Ben? Or was it a failure because Jo gave up her writing dream to marry? Did life need to be as absolute as Jo

March? Couldn't she be married and still write?

And then I wondered what my mother would think, were she still here. Would she consider me a failure if I did not try to attend the Academy? The thought brought tears in my eyes. My mother loved me deeply, and I knew she'd never think me a failure. Yet I still wanted to please her, even though she'd left us long ago.

Suddenly, James barged into my room limping from a knife wound he got playing that stupid game "mumblety-peg."

I frowned. "You forgot to knock."

He rolled his eyes and sat on the edge of my bed.

It was hard to believe James agreed to play that game. I mean, what in the world was he thinking? Father said it was lucky he wasn't playing with a bigger knife and that he'd been wearing shoes or he might have severed a muscle in his foot.

At least Father now joined me in questioning the wisdom of allowing James to play with Willie. Honestly, my brother needed more supervision.

"Are you going to the powwow?" James asked.

I sat up with a start. "Is it time?"

"Just about."

Not only was I planning to attend the powwow, my students were demonstrating their sketch work. I closed *Little Women* and set it on my bedside table, patting the cover. "I'll be back," I whispered.

James looked at me strangely. "Are you talking to your book?"

I pretended not to hear him. "I'll be ready in five minutes. Meet you downstairs."

I soon found myself on the fort's ramparts, without James, naturally, who disappeared with Willie hardly a moment after we arrived. The last I saw of that pair they were helping a very sweaty and portly photographer from Jacksonville carry his wooden tripod and boxy black camera around Fort Marion. It pleased me to see my brother being so useful for a change.

Lieutenant Pratt had asked me to hold an art class *en plein air* so tourists could see the men's sketch work. He said he was bringing a special tourist who was interested in buying some of the men's work.

I had asked Making Medicine, Boy Hunting, and White Horse to join me on the ramparts with their ledger books, and we began sketching and embellishing our drawings with colored pencils almost immediately. I sincerely hoped Lieutenant Pratt would come by soon because the men could not remain long. All three had informed me they needed to get ready to perform in the powwow.

We relaxed into our work, enjoying the sun and warming afternoon temperatures. Ben stopped by to say hello. "It looks more like St. Augustine, Oklahoma, than St. Augustine, Florida, at this fort today."

I laughed, knowing he was referring to the many small groups of Natives with blankets outstretched in front of their teepees, wearing their Native clothes and selling homemade trinkets. Even Ah-kah was wearing her buckskin dress, newly decorated with tiny shells tied to the fringe that jingled agreeably. She was selling her painted sea beans.

Lieutenant Pratt soon joined us, accompanied by a gentleman carrying a walking stick and wearing a top hat and silk tie. "Miss Callison. Mr. Broderick," Lieutenant Pratt nodded. "I'd like you to meet Tanner Landon of Atlanta."

I scrambled to my feet. Mr. Landon bowed. I curtsied, impressed. "How do you do, sir?" Ben shook the man's hand.

Lieutenant Pratt continued. "Mr. Landon read about our

Native artists in the newspaper up in Atlanta. Do you mind if he watches them work?"

"No sir, not at all," I said.

Mr. Landon stopped beside White Horse, who was intently coloring yet another white horse, this one with a few black spots. A native sat atop the horse, wearing a feather headdress and holding a spear while chasing a buffalo.

Clearly enthralled, Mr. Landon asked if he could hold the ledger book in order to examine it more closely. White Horse grudgingly handed it to him and waited impatiently for him to hand it back. Mr. Landon flipped through the pages and snapped the book shut.

"I'd like to purchase this book. Would five dollars be enough?"

White Horse did not speak perfect English, but he understood Mr. Landon's offer. He shook his head. Mr. Landon thought his denial a bargaining ploy. "All right, ten dollars then." Again White Horse shook his head. Mr. Landon seemed offended. White Horse grunted. "Not for sale," he said, reaching his hand up to get his book back.

But Mr. Landon held it tight. Instead, he pulled ten dollars plus another five dollars from a money clip inside his pocket. "Fine. Then fifteen dollars. That's my final offer."

Ben caught my eye. I could tell he thought I should encourage White Horse to accept the deal, but I knew better. This sketchbook was not a trinket to White Horse. It was a book of deep memories for a life he might never recover. I cleared my throat. "I fear, Mr. Landon, Chief White Horse does not want to part with his ledger book. But, some of our other artists might be willing to sell you their books."

I directed Mr. Landon toward Boy Hunting and we exchanged ledger books—Boy Hunting's book to Mr. Landon and White Horse's book back into the hands of its eager owner. "Boy Hunting is Kiowa, just like Chief White Horse. I believe he would love to sell you his book." Boy Hunting smiled and nodded.

Mr. Landon flipped through the pages. "This is excellent." He started to hand fifteen dollars to Boy Hunting.

"Oh, no sir," I said, feeling emboldened. "Boy Hunting's book sells for twenty dollars. He's an artist for his tribe, therefore his work costs more."

Mr. Landon gave me a withering look. He reached inside his pocket, pulled out another five dollars and handed the money to Boy Hunting.

Boy Hunting smiled and accepted it. "Ajo."

I translated for Mr. Landon. "That means 'thank you.'"

Mr. Landon tipped his hat and walked away. Lieutenant Pratt winked at me and followed Mr. Landon. Boy Hunting smiled widely. Ben looked at me, surprised. "When did you learn to bargain like that?"

I shrugged. "Just now." I joined Ben in a wide smile. He looked over my shoulder at Mr. Landon, now on the other side of the ramparts. "I think he's some sort of collector."

I nodded in agreement. Just then, White Horse reminded everyone it was time to go downstairs and prepare for the pow-wow. He and the Natives left while Ben and I walked downstairs to the courtyard to wait for the show to begin.

Chapter 19

Ah-kah, December 26, 1875

Ah-kah sold her box with the small violet shells to a pretty lady from Illinois for seventy-five cents. She was so excited she wanted to run to Hamblen's to buy licorice whips, but instead decided to stay to try and sell her sea beans. Her determination was rewarded when she sold all her sea beans for twenty-five cents apiece to a fancy-dressed man walking around with Lieutenant Pratt.

Ah-kah folded up her blanket and went inside the tent to count her money: two dollars and seventy-five cents. She hid it under her blanket, patting the blanket satisfactorily.

As she headed downstairs for the powwow, Ah-kah tried to decide how much she would give to Peonte to send to Kaku and how much she would spend on herself. She crossed the courtyard to the staging room for the powwow and looked up in time to see Bumpy Nose and Spotted Face chasing Tenequa through a warren of rooms. This did not really worry Ah-kah because she knew Tenequa could take care of himself. Besides, she needed to get the gourd she was assigned to shake during the powwow.

Tourists waited on benches that had been brought into the middle of the courtyard for the event. The benches formed a large square. In the center of it some men had arranged firewood in the shape of a small teepee. They put pine needles inside the teepee as a fire starter and Boy Hunting now lit the pine needles to signal the start of the powwow.

A Kiowa named Old Man walked slowly into the courtyard. Ah-kah and four others followed him. She carried a gourd partially filled with dried corn kernels, while the others carried a large drum. They all sat in a tight square not far from the fire with the drum in the middle. The men began beating a slow and complicated rhythm with their hands while Ah-kah accompanied them shaking the gourd. *Dum. Da-dum. Dum. Da—da-da-da-dum.*

Mrs. Mather stood on the edge of the courtyard behind the tourists. She caught Ah-kah's eye and nodded proudly at her student. Ah-kah allowed herself a small smile in Mrs. Mather's direction.

Four men crept into the courtyard from four different corners of the fort. They crawled on their hands and knees toward the center as if trying to enter unseen. One of the men was Pile of Rocks, a Comanche. Another was Bear Killer, a Cheyenne, and another was White Bear, an Arapaho. White Horse represented the Kiowa. They all looked warily from side to side as if on the prowl for some unseen enemy.

As she shook her gourd, Ah-kah watched like everyone else to see what the men would do next. When they got to the center, the Comanche and the Cheyenne squatted beside each other, exchanging hand signals. They joined forces and crept around the middle together. White Horse, the Kiowa, and White Bear, the Arapaho, did the same.

Ah-kah was sure the two groups would fight each other, and when they did, Pile of Rocks pretended to get badly hurt. All the men abandoned him, even his Cheyenne ally, Bear Killer. But just as it looked as if Pile of Rocks would die alone, flailing in pain in the dusty courtyard, Bear Killer returned to carry him away.

Ah-kah thought the dance a great show of loyalty. The tourists seemed to like it too. They clapped, and the four men returned to dance around the fire to the music. The drummers began chanting and more men joined in. Some had shells tied to their wrists and ankles that tinkled like tiny bells as they raised first one foot and then the other, twisting their bodies to the music.

When the powwow ended, Ah-kah sat on a bench and watched as tourists had their picture made with Black Horse and Lone Wolf. She felt sad that the powwow was over. It made her feel more homesick than she'd felt in weeks.

Ah-kah watched as the tourists walked toward the sally port to leave, including Bumpy Nose and Spotted Face. She blinked when she saw the boys. Ah-kah could hardly believe her eyes. Bumpy Nose carried a burlap sack slung over his shoulder, and it took her a moment to realize there was something inside that sack, something struggling to get out.

She frowned. No, she said to herself. They wouldn't. Just to be sure, she ran across the courtyard where she had last seen the boys chasing Tenequa. Her cat was nowhere to be found. She ran up the steps to the ramparts, knowing she would surely see him curled up in a ball on her blanket sound asleep. Ah-kah threw open the tent door. Tenequa was not inside. She ran to look over the fort's wall. There she saw the boys walking quickly toward the marsh, the sack bouncing heavily on Bumpy Nose's back.

Ah-kah tried to tell herself Tenequa could be anywhere in the fort. He was a mouser, after all, a hunter who followed his prey deep into the darkest corners of the fort. Still, she could not get rid of the nagging feeling of worry, which she felt as she pictured the sack, full of something quite alive, bouncing on the back of Bumpy Nose.

Ah-kah knew she had to do something. She ran back to the tent, grabbed her bow and arrows and headed out to follow those boys.

Chapter 20

Callie, December 26, 1875

I knew something must be amiss when I saw Ah-kah hurry-
ing through the courtyard toward the sally port, a bow slung
over her shoulder and her arrows sticking out of a thin rawhide
pouch on her back.

I elbowed Ben. "Where's Ah-kah going?"

Ben shrugged.

"I hope my brother has nothing to do with it." James had
been warned never to tease that poor girl again, but I did not
trust him. Not with that awful friend Willie by his side. "She
can't be going hunting."

"I'm sure it's nothing," Ben said.

"I'm going to follow her, just to be certain. Will you come
with me?"

"Sure," Ben said.

We hurried from the ramparts and through the sally port.
From the top of the bluff I could see Ah-kah walking purposely
along the seawall, the street beside her crowded as always with

horses, carriages, and tourists. We tried to catch up to her but were delayed when Ben ran into a hotel guest who asked for directions to the cigar shop. Ben politely explained how to find it, and we were on our way again.

"I can't see her anymore. Can you?" I asked standing on my tiptoes. Ben shook his head. We soon arrived at the end of the seawall and saw nothing unusual.

"Maybe she was just going to practice shooting. . . ."

Suddenly, a shriek filled the early evening air. "That sounds like one of the boys," Ben said, jumping off the seawall and crashing through the reeds. I followed. Moments later we found ourselves, muddy and breathless, standing in a clearing along the Matanzas River. I stared at Willie, who had an arrow jutting from his shoulder. An empty burlap sack lay on the ground near his feet. James stood close by, frozen to his spot. He seemed afraid to move. I didn't understand why until I turned to see Ah-kah, an arrow primed in her bow. It was aimed directly at my brother's chest.

"She shot me!" cried Willie, motioning toward Ah-kah with his chin.

It was then that Ben saw her as well. He raised his hand to try and get the girl to put down her bow and arrow.

"Bumpy Nose and Spotted Face tried to drown Tenequa," Ah-kah said, her words spitting from her mouth.

I whipped my head around to look at James.

"We just wanted to see if the cat could swim," he said defensively.

Ah-kah yelled. "You were getting ready to throw him into the water tied up in a sack. You would have killed him!"

My brother seemed like a stranger to me. I did not understand how he could be so mean.

Despite Ah-kah's primed bow, Ben walked over to look at Willie's shoulder. "Lucky she only shot you with a toy arrow," he said yanking the reed out of Willie. The boy screamed in pain.

Ben held his hand over the wound. "It wasn't in there that deep. You'll just need a stitch or two."

"She tried to kill me!" Willie cried.

"You tried to kill my cat," Ah-kah growled.

I took my cue from Ben and acted as if Ah-kah was not still standing tall, ready to shoot. I grabbed my brother's arm. "Say good-bye to your friend, James. This is the last time you'll run off with him, I can assure you."

I yanked my brother out of there and headed home for a serious discussion with Father. When we walked past Ah-kah she was trembling—from anger or fear, I'm not sure which. I knew Ben would resolve things, even though Ah-kah had aimed her bow and arrow at Willie again.

M.C. Finotti

Chapter 21

Ah-kah, January 13, 1876

Ah-kah walked through the sally port for the last time, her buckskin dress tinkling with each step. She stopped just outside the fort's gates to look at St. Augustine. She was surprised to realize she would miss this town.

Ah-kah carried two small bundles as she walked down the hill toward the waiting army wagon. Peonte followed close behind. Dick and Mrs. Mather waited for her at the bottom of the hill, along with Callie and her mean brother, Spotted Face. Ah-kah had no idea why that boy had come.

Although Bumpy Nose recovered quickly from his wound, his parents were quite angry their son had been shot by a Native girl with a bow and arrow. They met with Lieutenant Pratt and wanted Ah-kah charged with a crime, while Lieutenant Pratt argued that no crime had been committed. Ah-kah, meanwhile, had spent the last two weeks curled inside her teepee because naturally Peonte, Black Horse, and now even Lieutenant Pratt would not let her leave the fort.

Lieutenant Pratt finally told her parents he thought Ah-kah would be happier, not to mention safer, if she returned to the Oklahoma Territory. Mrs. Mather agreed. Eventually, so did her parents.

Now, Ah-kah was to travel back to Oklahoma with her mother. Peonte would deposit her with Kaku and her cousins and then return to St. Augustine to remain with Black Horse until the day the army declared that he, too, could return home.

When Ah-kah got to the bottom of the hill, Mrs. Mather hugged her tightly and then pressed a book into her hands.

"To practice your reading," she said.

"Thank you," Ah-kah said, quietly.

"If President Grant responds to your letter, I will send it to you in Fort Sill."

Ah-kah nodded, although she didn't hold much hope of a response anymore.

Dick hugged her next and spoke in Comanche. "As I already told you, that boy is lucky you only shot him in the shoulder."

Ah-kah's eyes began to water. She would miss Dick. She swallowed hard, forcing herself to be strong.

"Take care of Tenequa for me," she said, choking on the words in spite of herself. Tenequa had finally returned to the fort two days after the boys tried to drown him. He walked into Ah-kah's tent, plopped down beside her, and started purring. She was still thanking the Great Spirit for his safe return.

"Tenequa will miss you. He will have a long life, thanks to you," Dick said, smiling.

She quickly wiped her eyes with the back of her hand. She knew she'd miss Tenequa. She'd also miss selling sea beans to tourists. She had money in her pocket and black licorice whips in her bundle because of those sales. She couldn't wait to share her candy with Kaku and her cousins.

She also had the paintbrush and shells filled with paint color in the bundle too, along with several painted sea beans. In her other hand she carried molasses cookies made by Buffalo Calf and packed carefully in cloth so they would not break. She had promised the warrior woman she would give them to her children along with a big hug and kiss from their mother.

Spotted Face dug his toe in the dirt and mumbled, "I'm sorry."

Ah-kah frowned. She thought about asking him why he and his friend had been so mean to her, but she was determined not to care. Besides, Peonte hustled her away to the wagon before she had a chance to question him. A soldier had already opened the end gate and Peonte climbed in. Ah-kah followed.

The soldier slammed the end gate closed and the wagon pulled away almost immediately. Mrs. Mather waved. So did Dick and Callie. Ah-kah waved back, thankful that only Peonte could see her tears now, which flowed like a great river.

When they were out of sight, Ah-kah sighed and sat back. She wiped her eyes, slipped off the string from Callie's scroll and unrolled it. It was a watercolor painting of Fort Marion, with teepees atop the ramparts and the red, white, and blue flag of the Pale Face flapping in the breeze. The entire fort was set against a dawning sky painted in vibrant shades of blue and pink and yellow. It seemed alive with possibilities.

Ah-kah remembered the first time she saw Callie painting with those same colors. She thought of all she had learned since then. She could speak English now and read it. She could also write the Pale Face words. Most of all, she better understood the Pale Face and their ways. She wanted to help teach her people these same things.

But she knew she had changed in other ways as well.

Ah-kah felt closer to her father, a great Comanche fighter and chief, after spending so much time with him at the fort. Her father had taught her how to use a bow and arrow, which he never would have had time to do back home.

Ah-kah felt confident about her ideas now too. After all, the bows and arrows that she first started making were now big sellers at the fort. Painted sea beans were running a close second. Ahkah wanted to find a way to continue making things and selling them once she got home.

She let the painting roll up in her lap and smiled at the possibilities. She would paint her own dawn, one that didn't look anything like Callie's. Instead, it would be done in colors she alone would choose.

Chapter 22

Callie, January 13, 1877

Dear Ben,

It's happening! Snow is falling, gentle and white, covering Philadelphia in its silent embrace. I plan to remain snug in bed all day watching my first snowfall from this warm perch beside my bedroom window in Mrs. Coyle's Boarding House.

Luckily, it's Saturday and I don't have classes to attend because the walk to the Academy would be excruciating in this freezing weather. I now thoroughly understand why tourists flock to St. Augustine this time of year!

I cannot tell you how happy it made me to read in your last letter about a sponsor for Making Medicine. He is so eager to learn. I feel certain the sponsor's money will be well spent furthering his education. I am certain Mrs. Mather will find more benefactors to sponsor more of the men, as we both know how practiced she is in the art of getting what she wants.

There is a new teacher at the Academy who believes in verité, which means all students, including the ladies, must draw the human form from naked models. *If we are too nervous to do this he will allow us to use a plaster cast made from a naked model. I am not sure which I will choose yet, but I am leaning toward the plaster cast. I simply cannot imagine asking a model to take off her clothes and stand still for an hour in these freezing temperatures— no matter how big the stove in the room. That would pain me almost as much as it pained me to say goodbye to you and to father and to James five months ago.*

I still believe Ah-kah's departure from St. Augustine last year saved her, yet somehow it saved me too. She was so proud, so brave that day in her buckskin dress with the singing shells. I am sure she was scared—fear often walks beside change—but she was also determined to be as happy as she sounded.

In the end, I now know that attending the Academy was not just Mother's dream for me. It was my dream too. Thank you for understanding why I had to be brave and do this. Thank you for saying you will wait for me.

Love,
Callie

M.C. Finotti

Acknowledgments

Paintbrushes & Arrows is a work of fiction, although it was inspired by a true story. I owe a great debt of gratitude to the research of learned historians, particularly Professor Brad Lookingbill of Columbia College, Missouri, whose excellent book *War Dance at Fort Marion* was my "go-to" reference book for this novel.

I would also like to thank Carney Coffee Saupitty Jr. of the Comanche National Museum and Cultural Center in Lawton, Oklahoma. Mr. Saupitty, whose Comanche name is "The Time that Many Cheyenne Came Down to Make War On Us," or "Many Came," learned to speak Comanche when he was a boy. He is working hard to ensure this ancient and beautiful language remains alive for centuries to come.

Writers Kathryn Erskine, Beckie Weinheimer, Tricia Booker, and Nancy Stone read early versions of this novel and contributed valuable suggestions. A big thank-you to them and to artist Suzanne Hendrix for her cover art.

I would also like to thank June and David Cussen, who have worked tirelessly since 1982 to share the history of our great state with middle school students, teachers, Florida residents, and tourists. When someone complains that our state history doesn't amount to more than highways and shopping malls, I point them to *www.pineapplepress.com* and tell them to get reading.

Finally, I am grateful to my husband John, whose perpetual strength and grace has been my valued escort through life. All my love.

Historical Note

On May 21, 1875, Lieutenant Richard Henry Pratt arrived in St. Augustine with seventy-two Native American prisoners, and three non-prisoners, including a young girl whose name was recorded as Ah-kah, the daughter of Black Horse and Peonte. In Comanche, Ah-kah is a variation of "little girl."

Pratt's stated aim was to "kill the Indian and save the man." He organized daily life for the warriors at Fort Marion like a military unit, and allowed local churchwomen such as Sarah Mather to teach the warriors how to read and write. The churchwomen also introduced the Bible to the Native Americans, planting the seeds of Christian faith in many.

One of those Native Americans, the Cheyenne named Making Medicine, went on to become a baptized Episcopalian, who took the name David Pendleton Oakerhater. He eventually became an Episcopalian priest and opened a school and mission for Native Americans in Oklahoma. In 1985 the Episcopal Church designated this former warrior a saint. To this day many Cheyenne in Oklahoma call him "God's Warrior."

Lieutenant Pratt eventually rose to the rank of brigadier general. In the early days of his grand experiment, he actually provided art supplies and a painting teacher to work with Native American artists at the fort. The artists drew in ledger—accounting—books, which were often sold to tourists. This Ledger Art, as it has come to be known, is a source of great cultural pride for Native Americans today and has been preserved in universities and museums across the country. You can see fine examples of it online at *www.plainsledgerart.org.*

The prisoners stayed at Fort Marion three years. During the later years especially, Lieutenant Pratt gave them more freedom. He allowed the men to wear their Native dress and perform for the tourists. They made and sold trinkets to tourists, including bows and arrows. He also granted passes to the prisoners so they could leave the fort to work for the day, always returning by sundown. The passes allowed the men to clear land at nearby farms and ranches, stock shelves at stores in St. Augustine, and most importantly, send money back to their families in Oklahoma.

By 1878, the army deemed Lieutenant Pratt's bold experiment successful and the seventy-two prisoners were allowed to return home. However, a small group of the younger men who called themselves "The Florida Boys" chose not to return to Fort Sill. Sponsored by wealthy Christian benefactors, some went on to further their education at institutions of higher learning in Hampton, Virginia, and Syracuse, New York.

It is here that the real story of Ah-kah ends. She did not shoot anyone with a bow and arrow, nor was she forced to leave St. Augustine because of local bullies. Instead, letters written by some of the Florida Boys stated that she traveled to the Midwest with Lieutenant Pratt to meet a sponsor who would pay for her continued education. However, she got sick and went "home," likely to the reservation lands assigned to the Comanche in Oklahoma.

The army asked Pratt to expand his work and he started what would eventually be called the Carlisle Indian Industrial School in Carlisle, Pennsylvania. Native Americans often criticize this school, along with others modeled after it, because children were often forcibly taken from their homes and made to attend. While there they were punished if they spoke their Native tongue.

All of which brings us to Callison Crump, who sadly was not the painting teacher allowed to work with the Native Americans at the fort in 1875. This honor probably went to a man whose name is lost to history. Callie, however, is typical of a girl living in the South in the 1870s. Such a girl likely would have read *Little Women,* gone on to become a teacher if she was ambitious in that regard, and marry. There were not many other acceptable career choices for young women in that era.

One of biggest historical magnets throughout the centuries in St. Augustine has been the fort, which is now called the Castillo de San Marcos and is watched over by the National Park Service. The Castillo is the oldest fort in the continental United States and is the second oldest building in St. Augustine. (Only the Gonzales-Alvarez House is older.) It was called Fort Marion from 1825 to 1942. Construction on the fort began in 1672 and was finished in 1695.

Oh, the stories those coquina walls could tell! It is because of the pride and affection I feel for this one-of-a-kind monument that I donate fifty percent of the author proceeds from the sale of the book you now hold in your hands to the National Park Service in St. Augustine to be used as the NPS sees fit. Viva el Castillo! Viva St. Augustine!

Here are some other books from Pineapple Press on related topics. For a complete catalog, visit our website at *www.pineapplepress.com.* Or write to Pineapple Press, P.O. Box 3889, Sarasota, Florida 34230-3889, or call (800) 746-3275.

A Land Remembered, Student Edition by Patrick Smith. The sweeping story of three generations of MacIveys, who work their way up from a dirt-poor Cracker life to the wealth and standing of real estate tycoons. Volume 1 covers the first generation of MacIveys to arrive in Florida and Zech's coming of age. Volume 2 covers Zech's son, Solomon, and the exploitation of the land as his own generation prospers. Ages 9 and up.

The Treasure of Amelia Island by M.C. Finotti. This is the story of Mary Kingsley, daughter of former slave Ana Jai Kingsley, in 1813. Her family lived in La Florida, a Spanish territory under siege by patriots who see no place for freed people of color in a new Florida. Against these mighty events, Mary decides to search for a legendary pirate treasure with her brothers. Ages 8–12.

Escape to the Everglades by Edwina Raffa and Annelle Rigsby. Based on historical fact, this young adult novel tells the story of Will Cypress, a half-Seminole boy living among his mother's people during the Second Seminole War. He meets Chief Osceola and travels with him to St. Augustine. Ages 9–14.

Solomon by Marilyn Bishop Shaw. Eleven-year-old Solomon Freeman and his parents survive the Civil War, gain their freedom, and gamble their dreams, risking their very existence on a homestead in the remote environs of north central Florida. Ages 9–14.

The Spy Who Came In from the Sea by Peggy Nolan. In 1943 fourteen-year-old Frank Holleran sees an enemy spy land on Jacksonville Beach. First Frank needs to get people to believe him, and then he needs to stop the spy from carrying out his dangerous plans. Winner of the Sunshine State Young Reader's Award. Ages 8–12.

Blood Moon Rider by Zack C. Waters. When his Marine father is killed in WWII, young Harley Wallace is exiled to his grandfather's Florida cattle ranch. The murder of a cowman and the disappearance of his grandfather lead Harley and his new friend Beth on a wild ride through the swamps and into the midst of a conspiracy of evil. Ages 9–14.

Kidnapped in Key West by Edwina Raffa and Annelle Rigsby. Twelve-year-old Eddie Malone is living in the Florida Keys in 1912 when his father, a worker on Henry Flagler's Railroad, is thrown into jail for stealing the payroll. Eddie is determined to prove his father's innocence. But then the real thieves kidnap Eddie. Ages 8–12.

Olivia Brophie and the Pearl of Tagelus by Chris Tozier. Fantasy fiction. Olivia Brophie's dad has sent her to live with her eccentric aunt and uncle in the Florida scrub. Life is boring until Olivia slips down a tortoise burrow into the vast Floridan aquifer, where ancient animals thrive in a mysterious world. Age 8 and up.

Olivia Brophie and the Sky Island by Chris Tozier. Second book in the Olivia Brophie series. Olivia's life is in turmoil ever since she accidentally froze all of the earth's water and her aunt and uncle were kidnapped. With the help of a black bear named Hoolie, she must travel across America to undo the damage she caused. Age 8 and up.